Jane Gardam is the only writer to have been twice awarded the Whitbread/Costa prize for Best Novel of the Year, for *The Queen of the Tambourine* and *The Hollow Land*. She also holds a Heywood Hill Literary Prize for a lifetime's contribution to the enjoyment of literature. She is the author of five volumes of acclaimed stories: *Black Faces, White Faces* (David Higham Prize and the Royal Society for Literature's Winifred Holtby Prize); *The Pangs of Love* (Katherine Mansfield Prize); *Going into a Dark House* (Silver Pen Award from PEN); *Missing the Midnight* and, most recently, *The People on Privilege Hill*.

Her novels include *God on the Rocks*, which was shortlisted for the Booker Prize, *Faith Fox*, *The Flight of the Maidens* and the bestselling *Old Filth*, which was shortlisted for the Orange Prize in 2005.

Jane Gardam was born in Yorkshire. She now lives in east Kent and the Pennines.

Also by Jane Gardam

Fiction

The Summer After the Funeral
Bilgewater
Black Faces, White Faces
God on the Rocks
The Sidmouth Letters
The Pangs of Love and Other Stories
Crusoe's Daughter
Showing the Flag
The Queen of the Tambourine
Going into a Dark House
Faith Fox
Missing the Midnight
The Flight of the Maidens
Old Filth
The People on Privilege Hill
The Man in the Wooden Hat
Last Friends

For children

Bridget and William
The Hollow Land
A Few Fair Days

Non-fiction

The Iron Coast

Illustrated

The Green Man

JANE GARDAM

A Long Way
From Verona

ABACUS

First published in Great Britain by
Hamish Hamilton Ltd 1971
Published by Abacus in 1982
Reprinted 1984, 1985, 1986, 1987, 1989, 1990, 1992, 1993,
1994, 1995, 1997, 1999, 2004

This edition published by Abacus in 2009
Reprinted 2010, 2011, 2012, 2013

A CIP catalogue record for this book
is available from the British Library.

ISBN 978-0-349-12251-9

Typeset in Fournier by M Rules
Printed and bound in Great Britain by
Clays Ltd, St Ives plc

Papers used by Abacus are from well-managed forests
and other responsible sources.

MIX
Paper from
responsible sources
FSC
www.fsc.org   FSC® C104740

Abacus
An imprint of
Little, Brown Book Group
100 Victoria Embankment
London EC4Y 0DY

An Hachette UK Company
www.hachette.co.uk

www.littlebrown.co.uk

Contents

'The sun was shining on the sea,
Shining with all his might.
He did his very best to make
The billows smooth and bright.
And this was odd because it was
The middle of the night.'

Lewis Carroll
Alice Through the Looking Glass

Part I

The Maniac

I

I ought to tell you at the beginning that I am not quite normal, having had a violent experience at the age of nine. I will make this clear at once because I have noticed that if things seep out slowly through a book the reader is apt to feel let down or tricked in some way when he eventually gets the point.

I am not, I am glad to say, mad, and there is so far as I know no hereditary madness in my family. The thing that sets me apart from other girls of my age – which is to say thirteen – is that when I was nine a man wcame to our school – it was a private kindergarten sort of school where you could go from five upwards but most girls left when they were eleven unless they were really stupendously dumb – to talk to us about becoming writers. There weren't many of us who had really given a lot of thought to it – to writers at all, let alone to becoming them, and certainly not me, not in actual words and thoughts, that is. I had for a considerable number of years written things. There was always a lot of paper lying about in our house, my father being a school-master; and I can't really remember a time when I didn't

3

pick pencils up and write on it. It's funny but even now I don't think I could actually *buy* paper. It always seems to me as if it ought to be free. It's like parsons' children and collection. I steal paper sometimes when I'm not thinking.

Well this man came, and we all filed into the biggest classroom and the little ones sat down cross-legged upon the floor and the big ones lounged on chairs behind and then we were told to shush and the door opened and this terribly tired-looking man came in behind the Headmistress. 'Girls,' she said, 'this is Mr Arnold Hanger and he has come a very, very long way to talk to you on the subject of Becoming a Writer. Now I don't really need to intro*duce* you, Mr Hanger, because we all so *love* your books that we really (beam, beam) feel that we know you already.'

Then she said 'Mr Hanger' again rather sharply because he had his chin on his chest and looked as if he was dropping off. 'Mr Hanger,' she said, 'we feel that you are one of our very *oldest* friends.'

Everyone clapped like mad and biffed everyone else's knee and pushed at everyone else's elbow and snuffled, though keeping straight faces because of course NOBODY had ever heard of the man before except I suppose the Headmistress. I'm sure none of the other teachers had because they were all either too old to read anything at all any more or they hadn't started learning. It was a fairly peculiar sort of school.

The man looked as if he knew it too, and he just slowly lifted his eyelids up as the Head sat down and arranged herself, all powdery, with a modesty-vest and a very low, loose top half and looked up at him all hopeful. It was terribly funny somehow, and the girl sitting next to me and I collapsed and I nearly as anything had to go out. And I suppose my whole life would have been different if I had.

However.

Arnold Hanger got up with a deep sigh and looked all round us, and then his face broke into a great, lovely smile all over and he began to talk. And he was absolutely marvellous. Even the Top Form, the really ghastly ones who just sat about yawning all day and were going to do nothing when they left school but sit about yawning all day – it was a posh sort of school – even they sat up and listened.

He had a lovely voice and he had brought a lot of books with him with bits of paper stuck in to mark the place, and he kept picking up first one book and then another and reading bits out – long, long bits and sometimes very short bits. Poetry and all sorts.

Well, I was only nine and I wasn't really far off fairy tales. They had had a job getting me started reading at all actually, because I was always wandering about, making these scrawls on my father's foolscap, pressing my face against windows and so forth; WASTING TIME, as they all kept saying. He kept on – book after book after book that I'd never even heard of, poems and stories and conversations and bits of plays, all in different voices. And I sat so still I couldn't get up off the floor when it was over, I was so stiff.

The Head thanked him (beam, beam and BEAM) and he suddenly looked sad and tired again and went padding off after her to the door with his head down, while we clapped and clapped. He stood in the door with his back to us for a moment and then he turned round and stared at us; and suddenly he put up his hand and we were quiet.

'Thank you,' he said. 'I'm glad you enjoyed it. If there is anyone here this afternoon whom I have convinced that books are meant to be enjoyed, that English is nothing to do with duty, that it has nothing to do with school – with exercises and homework and ticks and crosses – then I am a happy man.' He turned away, but then he turned back again and he suddenly simply shouted, he *bellowed*. 'To hell with school,' he cried. 'To hell with school. English is what matters. ENGLISH IS LIFE.' The Head grabbed him and led him off to her sitting-room for tea, not looking too thrilled, and we were let out and I went flying home.

I got every one of my writings out of my desk and went tearing back again to the school gates – it was miles – but just as I got there I saw the station taxi creaking off and Mr Hanger's hat through the back window. I turned round and went flying off home again, through our garden and out the back to the railway line, and I looked both ways and ran across to the other side and along through the allotments on the railway bank until I came to the slope that led up to the platform, and I ran along it.

I was there before him and I had to wait until he came over the bridge.

He came very slowly. He had a brown pork-pie hat on and a long tweed coat, rather oldish. He stopped in the middle of the bridge to watch the train come in and look down the funnel and get covered in smoke like my father and I used to do when I was small, before my brother was born. And then very slowly, as if he didn't care whether he caught it or not, he tramped down the wooden steps of the foot-bridge towards the carriages. '*Come* along now,' the porter shouted, holding a third-class door open, 'look alive laddie,' and I rushed up just as he stepped in.

'Could you look at these?' I said. I pushed in front of the porter and flung all the bits of paper at him. 'Now then!' the porter said. There was a lot of waving and whistling and I could see Arnold Hanger scrabbling about on the floor inside, and then fighting with the leather strap that let the window down. He only got his head out as the train sailed off the end of the platform, but I managed to keep trotting alongside down the slope and he took off his hat and waved it very courteously, just missing the signal. 'Indeed yes. And where shall I return them?' he shouted, and I yelled back 'I've put my name and address in.' (Actually in those days I was apt to put my name and address on everything I wrote. I used to put it on all kinds of other things – particularly on my arms and thighs. I have noticed that this is a characteristic of children of that age.)

When I had had a bit of a to-do with the porter, and been shown out of the luggage entrance I calmed down a little and began to feel silly. I didn't tell anybody what I'd done and oddly enough nobody at school said much about the talk and neither did I. I watched the post for a day or two and then I rather forgot about it all, which is another thing that happens when you are eight or nine. Just as well because it was months and months later before I heard any more, right in the middle of winter. As a matter of fact it was on the day when we had to leave our house and go to live on the other side of England – 'in the vilest part of it', according to mother – because my father had decided to stop being a schoolmaster and to become a curate.

We were in the station taxi and mother was crying and Rowley, my brother, was crying too – he was still extremely young and it was about all he ever did – and my father was talking to the taxi man about whether there was going to be a war or not and trying not to look back at the house which still had all our curtains hanging in the windows, and the garden seats on the lawn, and even the swing in the pear tree because the house belonged to the school and most of the things had to be left for the next housemaster and his family.

I said, 'We ought to have taken the swing down. It'll rot if it's left out all winter,' and father said, 'Oh the Eaves's will take it down tomorrow. Great fellow, Eaves. He'll paint it and oil it and then store it in the loft. And he'll have the garden seats painted next spring I wouldn't wonder.'

'I like the garden seats peeling,' I said and then I started crying, too, and my father yelled, 'Great Scot! What's the matter with you all? Willy' (he always knows everyone's name), 'Willy, get your oars. Your taxi's afloat,' and he got his handkerchief out and blew his nose very loudly and then dusted the nostrils violently east to west until his eyes watered.

As he put the handkerchief away he said, 'Here, Jessica, I forgot to give it to you. There was a letter for you today,' and as the taxi stopped he put into my hands a long, fat envelope typewritten in bright blue and addressed to me.

I opened it straight off in the little alley where we had to queue up for our tickets and dropped a whole lot of things that I was supposed to be carrying because mother had Rowley and the baby-bag and a lot of parcels (she is a terrible packer). 'Jessica,' she said. 'Must you read *now*?' and I didn't answer but just looked because there were all my writings again and on the top of them Mr Hanger had pinned a piece of paper and in bright blue typewriting he had said:

JESSICA VYE YOU ARE A WRITER
BEYOND ALL POSSIBLE DOUBT!

2

This experience changed me utterly, like Heaven, 'in the twinkling of an eye', and I believe is the reason for the next point I have to make clear before getting on with the story. Which is that I am not really very popular. Some people in fact do not really like me at all. In fact if you really want to know quite a lot of people absolutely can't stand me.

I'm not just saying it and trying to cadge sympathy like they say eldest children do when they are displaced in their parents' affections by the birth of a second child. I'm not in the least bit jealous of Rowley. You couldn't be jealous of him. He's sweet although he's terribly spoilt and gets away with everything they used to go for me like anything for (I am fond of putting prepositions at the end of sentences, as in fact was Shakespeare).

The thing I can't understand though about being unpopular is that people often start by liking me very much. You can see. For instance when we moved from father's school to this place, Cleveland Sands, and I was sent to the High School at Cleveland Spa I was terribly popular. I was chosen as form captain my very first term and even rounders captain although I'm hopeless, and everyone wanted me for their partner in team games and skipping and train-line. Then it slowly all faded away and they seemed to start hating me as much as they had liked me. It was awful. You could see them curling their lips and turning away and sniggering. I didn't know what to do about it. I even got three bags of toffees — it was before rationing — and handed them round everyone saying, 'Take two, I've got heaps,' but they all just looked at me as if I were mad and said 'Thank you,' watching me while they dipped their hands in, and I heard them all laughing about it afterwards. Florence Bone — she's my friend — said 'Why do that?' and I didn't say anything. Then I said, 'Why does everyone *hate* me so?' and she said, 'They don't. What's the matter with you? Calm down.' She is very calm and steady, Florence Bone, and terribly good at Mathematics and very truthful as a rule.

But she wasn't being truthful then. I knew they didn't really like me and except for Florence there wasn't any one of them I really liked either, so I don't know why I cared. 'I can't see why you expect so much,' Florence said. 'We like you all right. What on earth do you *want*?'

But she was telling lies. There is this other thing I have to explain about myself which will show that she was telling lies: and that is that I have this power of knowing what people are thinking. I'm not boasting about it. Honestly, it is just something I was born with. As a matter of fact it's not all that uncommon. I have met one or two other people who can do it. I met one last year and you will hear about her and much good will it do you because she was the ghastliest woman . . . But that is not the point at the moment.

The point is this – in three parts. Tripartite. Viz:

1. I am not quite normal
2. I am not very popular
3. I am able to tell what people are thinking.

And I might add

4. I am terribly bad at keeping quiet when I have something on my mind because
5. I ABSOLUTELY ALWAYS AND INVARIABLY TELL THE TRUTH.

I am honestly not being conceited about this (No. 5). It is something I cannot help. There is nothing good about doing a thing if you can't help it. It is more like an illness than anything. Florence Bone says that really I ought to see a psychiatrist about it and I even asked my father if he thought so too. All he did though was snort like mad and say that I needed a psychiatrist less than anyone he'd ever met.

Incidentally this business of having to tell the truth has absolutely nothing to do with my father being a curate.

When I had been at Cleveland Spa for simply ages and was twelve years old I thought it would be a good idea to do something at the end of the term, like going out to tea or something. There was a tea shop called Elsie Meeney's on the corner of Ginger Street which we passed every day on the way from the station (Cleveland Spa is ten miles from Cleveland Sands). It was a very dark shop with a glass canopy outside it over the pavement, held up with posts. Before the war there had been baskets of flowers hanging between the posts, giving it all an air, and you could still see the metal baskets hanging though there were no flowers in them. The canopy thing had had the glass taken out because of air-raids and was boarded up.

The windows in this shop had slanting cake-shelves in them with circles of paper at intervals where cakes should have been. There was a notice saying 'Weddings a Speciality' and two oldish teacakes lying in a corner. Already, though the war had only been on a bit more than a year, cake shops were beginning to look much too big.

'*Do* they do teas?' Helen Bell asked. 'They don't look as if they do anything.'

'Yes they do,' I said, 'I found out. I went in one dinner hour and I asked. I said, "Do you serve afternoon teas?" and they said "Well I suppose so," and there's a notice inside pinned up actually saying "teas".'

The three of them – there were Helen Bell, Florence Bone and this peculiar girl, Cissie Comberbach – looked as if they would believe it when they saw it and we all filed into the shop and rested our shoe bags and gas masks and satchels on the floor, putting our report envelopes in our mouths while we did it. There was a thin woman behind the counter in a lavender overall reading a magazine. Now and then she gave a colossal great sniff and turned a page. Florence gave me a push. 'Go on then,' she said. I coughed.

The woman didn't look up. She turned a page and flexed her feet and I coughed again.

'Excuse me,' I said, 'may we have some tea?'

'Eh?' she said.

'Tea,' I said.

'*Tea?*' she said.

'Yes,' I said. 'Like it says.'

'Well I don't know,' she said. She looked hard at the card. It was pinned to an archway where two long red plush curtains were caught back in the middle at the top of the three steps.

'It does *say* tea,' Florence said, not to the woman though, just to the air round about.

'Oh well I dare say it *says* tea,' she said and sniffed. She turned over a page of the magazine and flexed her feet round and round.

'Well I did ask and it *says* tea and we're going in,' I said.

We stamped in under the archway up the steps and sat down in a small round room with a stained glass window in the back with strips of brown sticky paper stuck all over it in a lattice in case of bombs. It was a very stuffy room and there were only two tables in it. One was a big round table with a dirty cloth on it and the other was a little table with a clean cloth on it and a notice saying 'Reserved'. We sat down at the dirty table. Helen and Cissie looked at each other and Cissie sniggered.

'Now we order,' I said. 'We ask for a menu.'

'If there is one,' said Florence. 'We've got a hope.'

It grew very quiet.

'Look,' said Helen after a while, 'why did you want to *come* out to tea? I can't see what you *wanted*.' She has narrow hands and a narrow face, Helen Bell. She is good at playing the piano. On the whole I don't like people who are always playing the piano. They have mean little mouths.

'Well,' I said, 'it's an outing, isn't it? It's nice. It's something to do at the end of term. My mother often used to take me out to have biscuits and lemonade in tea shops where we lived before. It was just a cheerful thing to do, that's all.'

'We'll miss the train home.'

'Well we can get the next. That'll be even nicer.' We'd had all this out before I may say, we'd discussed it for hours. We'd got permission – letters from our mothers and a shilling each and everything. The way they plugged on at things at this school! It takes them ages to get on and *do* anything. There is a lot of Danish blood on this part of the coast my father says, and the Danes tend to stand about rather. After all, look at Hamlet.

'They think I'm crazy at home,' Helen said. 'I've told them to keep my tea hot.'

'But this *is* your tea. Proper tea. Little eclairs and things. Afternoon tea.'

'Where?' asked Helen.

'Well, in a minute,' I said.

'Are you crazy?' Cissie Comberbach said (she hardly ever spoke). 'There's a war on.'

'It's not been on that long. If there's still tea shops there's still teas. You just don't know round here anything about it. It used to be marvellous in places like this, people in coloured hats eating ices, and flowers hanging and lovely fat chocolate biscuits and the sun!' Helen turned her face away and picked her gas mask up and swung it about as if she would soon be going, and I suddenly felt absolutely fed up with her.

'AHEM,' I shouted. We really DO NEED THE MENU. Do you think we could please have a MENU.' (I used my mother's voice when she suddenly thinks I USED TO BE A HOUSEMASTER'S WIFE!)

Through the curtains in the shop the woman clattered down off her stool and came and stood in the archway. 'We don't have any menu,' she said curiously. She kept her finger in the magazine and looked at us. Then she shouted 'Allus!' Far away there was an answering call and a fat untidy woman slopped up into view at the back of the dark dining-room, through some hole in the floor so far as we could see. She seemed surprised to see us. 'We're shut,' she said, and prepared to vanish.

'You're not,' I said. 'I asked yesterday. We've got permission. And anyway there's a clean table-cloth laid over there with reserved on it.'

'That's a regular. 'Op it.'

'We won't. We've got the money. We've come for tea.'

'If you don't 'op it I'll send for the p'lice.'

'If you don't bring us our tea, *I'll* get the police,' I said, 'because you have advertised something you haven't got.'

Florence kicked me under the table. 'Shut up,' she said. 'You've gone all red. We'll go.' The others were already getting up and picking up their things. I said, 'We're stopping.'

'Oh come on, we're going,' said Helen.

'We're stopping here,' I said in my mother's voice and then unfortunately I knocked over a very large and heavy seaweed-green round plant pot on the top of a sort of bamboo thing behind my chair. It fell on its head. You'd never have believed the crash.

'Me busy-lizzie,' the lavender-aproned one shrieked.

I said, 'We're stopping.'

'Oh all right then, stop,' said the fat woman. 'But I'll tell you one thing. It's only rum balls. No fancies.'

We waited. Cissie Comberbach kicked the soil about under her feet and Helen said, 'I don't think I like rum balls.'

I said, 'If they're alcohol I *will* tell the police. She's not allowed to give alcohol to children.' Florence said, 'Never mind alcohol. You never asked how much it'd be. She didn't say. We ought to have got it straight. I mean we've only got a shilling each. I haven't any extra, have you?'

I hadn't. Helen had fourpence and Cissie Comberbach had a penny. We had railway passes to get home with.

'Let's call her back.'

'Help, no.'

'We'd better. We'd be in a mess.' Florence went over to the mantelpiece and pinged a bell like a metal muffin. After a while the counter woman shouted through, 'What's it this time then?'

'We want a *shilling* tea,' Florence said.

'Ho, you do, do you?'

I said, 'Florence you couldn't have!'

'What?'

I said, 'You *couldn't* have asked for that!'

'Why not?'

'Well it's awful. 'A shilling tea'. It sounds awful. It sounds coarse,' I said.

'Why's a shilling tea coarse?'

'It just is. Like "a meat dinner",' I said.

'I wouldn't say no to a meat dinner,' she said. 'Let's go. They're awful people here.'

The fat woman rose up through the floor and slapped a tray in front of us. ''Ere's yer rum balls,' she said, 'bread an' butter, marg., that is, pineapple jam, teacakes, potter tea for four, four cups, sugar.'

'Is it a *shilling* tea,' Florence asked.

'Shilling! Huh!' she said and went.

Helen sighed and said, 'So what do we do? We don't know if it's a shilling whatever happens or it's so much according to what we eat.'

But Cissie had started. 'We'll eat something,' Florence said. 'We'll just not eat it all in case. Actually I don't think I could eat more than one rum ball.'

Helen said that she didn't think she would be able to lift more than one off the plate. She said she thought they were made out of the soil of the plant pot which for her was an absolutely stupendous joke. Cissie even laughed at it, or tried but was unable to force open her teeth. I began to laugh and unfortunately knocked the teapot over and it began to pour about all over the tablecloth and into the teacakes and then slowly began to pour on to the floor with a very rude splashing noise and Florence suddenly started to howl like a dog.

'O lor' now I've done it. I'd better ping the thing.'

'No, mop it up.' Helen handed over her science overall. 'The cloth was filthy to start with.'

'I didn't want any teacakes,' Florence said kindly. 'Actually I think it's softened them up a bit.'

'Good job there's no one else here.'

'You'd not have made such a mess if there had been.' (Florence had recovered herself.) 'You'd have been more careful.'

'You'd of be'aved,' said Cissie.

'We're the only ones that've ever been here, I should think.'

'I expect the odd bod comes in,' Florence said. 'And odd is what they'd have to be.'

The bell on the shop door rang out, a voice cried 'Coooeee!' and feet tapped and a woman came up the steps into the tearoom, a woman who was the most dreadful colour – dark yellow, and her face all painted with paints. She had removed her eyebrows so that she had only shiny semi-circles and had painted other black semi-circles above them. She had a painted curly mouth like a doll and wore a band low down on her head like a Red Indian. Her clothes hung down from the shoulders and were looped up with a belt well below the waist and she had old pointed shoes on with buttons. On her poor old arms she had a lot of amber bangles hanging. There was something about her that made you think you'd seen her before somewhere. She was like someone your mother knew when you were young. She was very old. Her arms were quite wasted away. 'The rainbow comes and goes,' she said. 'And lovely is the rose.' She sat down at the clean table and nodded across, and smiled.

'Churchill is speaking tonight,' she said. 'Winston. He may be Churchill to all the world but he's Winston to me.'

'Gosh,' I said. 'D'you know him?'

Helen said, 'Shut up, don't talk to her. For heaven's sake!'

'Know him! Of course I do. Known him for years. Oh I wish I were in dear old London.'

'Did you know him when he was young or something?'

'He's not old,' she said. 'He's my age.'

The others put their faces in their cups.

'Churchill to all the world but Winston to me,' she went on as the counter lady came up without her magazine and began to flap a clean napkin over the shiny white tablecloth. The fat woman, Alice, appeared and put a tray down in front of her. 'There you are, Mrs 'Opkins then,' she said in a different, sweet, bright sort of voice. 'Lovely day. Just a bit of a fret. Your usual, dear?'

'Winston to me,' she said lighting a cigarette and putting it in a great long green holder. 'I've known them all.'

'Look at her tea,' Helen said. 'Crippen, just look at her tea.'

On the tray were little cress sandwiches and egg ones — even egg ones — three slices of fresh bread and butter, thin and curled like cornflakes, quite fresh, and a chocolate eclair in pale green paper. There was a tiny glass dish with blackcurrant jam in it. We sat and we looked. We looked and we looked and we went on looking.

She dropped ash on the bread and butter and poured herself some tea. She stared into space. 'I've known them all. Every mother's son of them,' she said. 'Henry James...'

Helen said, 'Where on earth does a tea like that *come* from?'

'I suppose you can get it if you pay,' said Florence.

'What?' I said.

'Well of course you can. You don't expect Churchill and the King and so on to eat rum balls and muck, do you?'

I said of course they did.

'Gaarn,' said Cissie. 'Never 'eard of the Black Market?'

'It's not Black Market,' Florence said. 'If you're a restaurant or a tea-shop or something you get an allowance. In posh places you get posh things. Like grouse. There's plenty of grouse and stuff if you can pay. You don't expect dukes and things to eat rum balls.'

'I don't believe it,' I said. 'I don't believe it of the King. He keeps to his rations. I read it. And he's ploughing up Buckingham Palace for vegetables.' (I was still pretty young.)

'That'll be to feed the cooks,' said Florence.

'I am absolutely certain,' I said, 'of the King.'

'I suppose you know him,' said Helen.

'I know them all,' said the woman across the room, staring ahead of her through the archway at the quiet, drizzly road. She stubbed out her cigarette in the eclair and pushed her plate away. 'Now I don't suppose you girls even know who Henry James was?'

'The Old Pretender,' I said. It was polite to have a go.

'That's her,' said Florence. Cissie collapsed. So did I as a matter of fact, but Mrs Hopkins didn't appear to notice.

'He was a Man. He was more than a Man, he was a Mind.

He was a great and civilized Mind. He loved England. He understood England. He even lived in England.'

'Well we all live in England,' I said.

'Shrup,' said Florence, 'I think he must have been an American.'

'The Old Pretender was a Scotsman.'

'The Old Pretender was *not* the same as Henry James,' said Florence.

'Why wasn't he?' I said, getting angry.

'He was Henry James to all the world,' said Mrs Hopkins. 'But he was Harry to me.'

'Oh, Henry Fifth,' I said. 'God for Harry.' It was something my father was always saying.

'WHAT did you say?' For the first time Mrs Hopkins seemed to see us. 'You, child, what did you say?'

'I said "God for Harry",' I said uncomfortably, and then I added, 'England and St George.' I shouldn't have.

'My dear child!' she cried, 'my dear child! That's what I thought you said. My *dear* child!' and she came tweedle-deeing over the room and kissed me! There was a terrible old smell about her like chests of drawers, and I shuddered and pressed back and nearly sent the busy-lizzie going for the second time. 'Well, would you believe it!' she said, '"God for Harry, England and St George". My dear children, might I just shake you by the hand? I'm going to write this down. Every word. I'm going to send it to the papers. I'm going to send it to Winston. Now would you mind if I were just to ask you your ages?'

'Around twelve,' said Florence, watchfully.

'And thirteen,' said Helen.

'My dears! Oh, my dears, how lovely. On the threshold. Four little Juliets. Younger than she are married mothers made! My dears, I want to repay you. Repay you just for being what you are. Little English Juliets. Lovers of dear old England. Now, I'm going to tell Winston about all this.' She spotted Helen's roll of music under the table. 'And what's this, you play music, too — what's this? Chopin? No! This has been a wonderful afternoon. Oh I do wish I could thank you *dear* children for it in some way.'

She shook hands all round and went off. We heard her saying 'Chopin, Grace,' to the counter lady, 'Chopin! He may have been Chopin to all the world but he was . . .'

'Quick,' said Florence, 'get her tea.'

We divided sandwiches, eclair, bread, butter, jam, sugar lumps. In less than two minutes there were none of them to be seen.

'Come on,' said Helen. 'Let's pay and go. Ping the thing. Good heavens.'

But the fat one, Alice, was already in the room. 'Now then?' she said.

'We'd like to pay,' I said.

'You'd like to pay.' She looked intently at Mrs Hopkins' empty tray. 'You'd like to pay. Mrs 'Opkins made a good tea today, Grace.'

'Paid 'er usual,' called Grace. Alice looked at us suspiciously. 'Four shilluns,' she said.

Florence, Helen and Cissie each put their shilling on the table and I began to look in my satchel.

'*Four* shilluns,' she said. 'That's one shillun *each*.'

'I can't just . . .' I said, 'just for the moment . . .' Florence said, 'Look in your gas mask.' I looked in my gas mask and took out my identity card, sweet coupons, stones, string, a drawing, a first-aid book, a bandage, a twig, a photograph, handkerchiefs and so on, and she just stood.

'I know I *had* it. I had it loose. It wasn't in a purse. I had it when I came in.' She put her hands on her hips and turned her mouth ends down like a tortoise. 'Now we're in a mess,' said Florence.

'I'll need the other shillun.'

'Oh crikey,' I said.

'They're short on a shillun, Grace.'

'Oh go on!' Grace called unexpectedly.

'Eh?'

'Go on! They're paid up. She paid.'

'*She* paid. Mrs Loony 'Opkins. She paid her pound and five bob over. For the girls, too, she said.'

We stared. 'Talk about luck,' said Florence. 'That was pretty kind when you think of it.'

'She was rich,' said Helen.

'Yes, but kind.'

'Darft,' said Cissie, the only thing she'd said for ages.

'Well thank heavens she was. We'd have been in a mess. We'd have had to go to the police. Gaoled for all I know.'

'No we wouldn't,' I said. 'I've found it. It was in my sock.' We were outside now. 'What did she mean "Four Juliets" and "married mothers"? Did she really think we were married mothers? Juliet wasn't married, was she?' (I honestly didn't know.)

Florence said perhaps she was an unmarried mother and Helen raised her eyebrows. 'Married to the Old Pretender,' I said and Cissie actually laughed. We were all suddenly in a very good mood and we ran down under the subway, screaming a bit. Cissie fell over.

'It was worth it,' I said. 'I told you it'd be worth it. It was worth the shilling.'

'What you haven't realized,' said Florence, 'what you haven't grasped' (she had on her Mathematics face) 'is that we've still *got* the shilling. We have all still *got* a shilling. We can all have chips.'

3

I have described the outing to Elsie Meeney's very carefully and in the fullest detail as it has a good deal of bearing on what happened next, though you might not think so at first. And, though I should never have guessed myself, it linked up with a very important and dreadful day at the beginning of the next term.

It was September. We'd had a lovely summer holiday in spite of the air-raids and Dunkirk and everything and I seemed to be getting on better with people rather. So I went back to school very cheerful and did a lot of fooling about. No one was as surprised as I was – and I'm still surprised as a matter of fact now – to hear that Cissie Horrible Comberbach had overheard our form-mistress Miss Dobbs telling Miss Somebody Else in the staffroom that Jessica Vye was getting above herself and needed a bit of setting down. Cissie had been waiting outside the staffroom for Miss Dobbs's case – she hears an awful lot, being so quiet – and she told Helen Bell about it in the shoe-bags, and Helen told me.

All I thought at the time, or all I thought I thought was

'Never mind. She'll have read my essay by this afternoon.'
Later on I knew that I had actually been very hurt by it.
'She'll soon have read my essay,' I thought and turned away
looking as if I didn't care at all.

In Scripture it was quite obvious that Miss Dobbs was on
the watch and I thought it again. She kept jumping questions
at me and spinning round quickly from the board to try and
catch me out. When she saw I was just writing away she
turned back to the board with a heavy face. Florence flicked
a pellet across. 'What's the matter?' she said. I just went
steadily on, writing out old Shalmaneser's dates and looking
very controlled.

'Were you talking, Jessica?'

'No, Miss Dobbs.'

'Are you sure?'

'Yes, Miss Dobbs.'

'Well I'm not.'

'It was me, Miss Dobbs.'

'"It was I",' said Miss Dobbs. (She is a confusing
woman.) 'Then stop.'

So I thought for the third time, 'She'll have read my essay
by this afternoon.' Miss Dobbs had not seen any of my
essays before. We hadn't done any essays last year in the
thirds.

At break we all filed out across the road on to the promenade. We were a double line marching left, right, straight
ahead and then fountaining out, running all over the green
grass. Everyone began to shout and play, and the little new

girls began to skip on the asphalt paths splashing up and down in the big shallow shining puddles. They began to chant 'Salt, mustard, vinegar, pepper' and other rhymes at the top of their voices. There was a girl at each end of a rope and six or eight girls in between, all jogging and chanting in the sunshine, four or five ropesful.

One lot chanted:

'When the war is OVER, Hitler will be DEAD,
He hopes to go to HEAVEN with a halo on his HEAD.
But the Lord said NO
You'll have to go BELOW
There's only room for CHURCHILL
So cheery-cheery OH!'

'Wait till this afternoon,' I thought again and I looked over the wire down at the North Sea flowing in, miles and miles of waves, all rose-pink in the sun. There were some ships – the tail of a convoy – disappearing over the horizon far away, and nearby but far below down the cliffs there were great black iron sword-things stuck in the sand. Excaliburs. Miles and miles of mines were hidden on the empty beaches with the cold wind blowing and the rosy sea. 'Just wait,' I thought. 'Wait till she reads it. She's probably reading it now, or in the dinner hour.'

It was double Maths after break and easy because it was L.C.M.s which are things that I can do. Florence did hers in her head and had finished in about four minutes. She flicked a pellet across.

'Was that you, Jessica?' This was Miss Pemberton (nice). It looked as if they'd been getting her on to me too.

'No, Miss Pemberton.'

'Are you sure?'

'Yes, Miss Pemberton.'

'Well I'm not.' (They're not all that original, our staff on the whole.)

'Please, Miss Pemberton, it was me.'

'"It was I". Did you want something?'

'Yes,' said Florence. 'I've finished.'

'Then here is another pageful.'

Florence took it and began to write down all the answers. Soon we set off for dinner.

The Junior School is about half a mile from the Senior School. It is a big ugly old house on the sea front, and except for prayers at the beginning and end of every term the juniors stay in it all the time. There are only four forms of juniors – three forms of the new girls and one form of girls left over from the year before who are sort of senior-juniors. This form is there (1) To set an example to the new girls, (2) For the girls who are still nearer twelve than thirteen, and (3) For the girls who don't at the moment seem to be very clever. Helen Bell, for example, was there because of (1), Florence Bone was there because of (2), and I was there because of (3). Nobody quite knew why Cissie Comberbach was there. Or anywhere.

Every day at the Junior School there is dinner for fourpence. It is usually a plate of brown liquid with potatoes, followed by a plate of white liquid with a blob of jam in the middle. If your parents thought it worth the money, however, you could walk up every day to have a better dinner for a shilling at the Headmistress's house across the road from the Senior School. Florence and I did this with one or two other girls and there were about twenty girls altogether when you got there – huge girls like women. Very stately.

'Did you know,' I asked Florence on the way there this particular day, 'that Miss Dobbs is trying to set me down a bit?'

Florence said she didn't.

'Well she is. Helen heard her say so. She's trying to get me an order mark.'

Florence is a very interesting girl. She doesn't just gasp sympathetically at things, always agreeing with you to your face like a lot of people. She is not easily excited and is able to weigh things up. Sometimes she finds that they do not in fact weigh anything at all, even though other people are simply groaning under them. This is often very comforting, and it was now. She walked along without speaking for a while and then she said, 'Oh, she is, is she. Then we'll sing her a song.' And she began singing in a very deep voice. The sound came out of her great wide face, deep and fruity. It is difficult to describe how absolutely funny she was. We all collapsed and people passing by drew back from us because we were all over the pavement. I felt much better.

It was brambles for pudding, with or without custard. Lovely. But then Florence found a little worm. It had eaten so many brambles that it had turned purple throughout. It was quite dead and she laid it on the edge of her plate. Then she looked and found another and another, and arranged them round her plate and everybody stopped eating. I went cold. 'I shall die,' I said, and turned sideways.

'Hello,' said Miss Birdwood, the Headmistress's friend who ran the shilling dinners. 'Hello, what's the trouble?'

I said with my eyes shut, 'Worms.'

'Nonsense,' she said. 'How dare you, Jessica. They are beautiful brambles. The Headmistress and I picked them ourselves upon the Whins. Where are the worms? Have you actually *seen* any worms? Now look at your plate.'

I looked and it all seemed worms.

'Finish your pudding.'

'I can't.'

'Rubbish.'

'I'd rather die.'

'Very well.' She quietly put down the tablespoon. 'I shall have to go and tell Miss LeBouche.'

Miss LeBouche, the Headmistress, was hardly ever seen by Juniors. She was just someone on a platform three times a year or so, misty and not very loving. A bit like God was to Shalmaneser. Not friendly. She had her dinner on a tray in her sitting-room every day – or we supposed so. We never heard a sound.

Miss Birdwood went out and after a minute came back with her lips pursed together, not looking at anyone, only at the purple brambles on the sideboard. 'Jessica Vye,' she said. 'Miss LeBouche has said you are to have an order mark.'

'Miss Birdwood, it was me,' said Florence.

'"It was I". Don't be silly, Florence, of course it wasn't.'

'It was. I've got thousands. I expect I got the nest or something.'

'STOP! That will do. Now then. Second helpings?'

Nobody seemed to want second helpings. 'Then, For what we have received . . .' Chairs scraped. 'May we be truly thankful. Amen.'

'Bother Buggy Birdwood,' said Florence, 'I wish she'd buggy-off,' and everyone collapsed, even the big girls, even Iris Ingledew who was going to Cambridge next year if she got a scholarship which she would. Miss Birdwood looked terribly bewildered – actually she's all right Miss Birdwood – and gave me a very stern and sorrowful look as we filed out.

We set off back to the Junior School in a queer excited mood. Cissie Comberbach, who is usually the colour of mashed potatoes, had gone quite pink. She is a very very small girl and as I've said before she hardly ever speaks. If you had to think of one word to describe her you would say, 'watchful'. She's funny. She was evacuated from London or somewhere to an aunt's farm near Kirkhinton Beck because of the air raids with a terribly long journey to school on about seventeen different buses. She looked terribly tired half the time. You could tell what a stupid sort of family she must have had to send her to a place like Teesside to get away from air raids. We were getting air raids just about every night.

Anyway she was fearfully thrilled about my order mark.

'You're the very first of all of us to get an order mark,' she said.

'If you get three,' said someone else, 'you get a conduct mark, and if you get two conduct marks you are expelled.'

Florence began to sing.

> 'All chequered were the skies,
> Ozymandias!'

She makes songs from titles and first lines of Palgrave's Golden Treasury, and we were writing a small opera in this way.

Cissie sidled up to me. 'What'll your parents say if you're expelled?' she asked.

'Oh come on,' said Florence, 'she's only got one *order* mark.'

I balanced myself along somebody's garden wall, and looking very unconcerned, I began to hop upon one leg. 'Salt, pepper, vinegar, mustard,' I said. 'When the war is OVER, Hitler will be DEAD. Let's play dares.'

'What, going into houses?'

'Yes.'

'What's that?' asked Cissie. She hadn't been in our lot last year. She'd started tagging on to Helen Bell at the end of the summer term which was the only reason I'd invited her to the party at Elsie Meeney's. 'What's going into houses?'

'Well, it's choosing a house and going and knocking on the door and asking if Mrs Something Funny lives there — somebody peculiar-sounding but not so peculiar-sounding that they guess, and they say no, and you say, but they *said* it was this address, and they get all puzzled and rack their brains.'

'What exactly is it *for*?' asked Cissie.

'I must say I do rather wonder,' said someone. 'We used to think it was terribly funny last year. It's a bit dishonest really.'

'No it's not,' I said. 'They like it. It gives them something to think about. They're all just resting after their dinners. They must get terribly bored, their husbands all in the army and their children at school. Come on, let's go down The Cut.'

'We're not allowed.'

'Oh fiddle.'

'We're not. We have to keep to the same way, Norma Crescent, Station Approach, under the subway and Ginger Street.'

'I've never seen why,' I said. 'I like The Cut. There's absolutely no reason why. It's just as quick . . .' While they wrangled on I thought, 'We'll still be back in time. She'll have read my essay now. She'll be passing it round the staffroom . . .' I seemed to see her, so clear that I could have touched her, sitting upright all of a sudden, after opening my book. 'My word, Amy, look at this!' And turning back to look at the name on the cover, 'Good heavens! It's Jessica Vye! It's marvellous.' 'Come down The Cut,' I said.

We went down The Cut which is a curving road going downhill as it curves. The houses are of funny white brick, all points and pinnacles. The people in the houses at the top end can see the sea flashing beyond the allotments even from their sitting-rooms but at the bottom end only from the attics. Each house has a long narrow garden in front.

'This one'll do,' I said. 'Whose turn is it?'

'Cissie's never.'

'All right. I dare you, Cissie.'

'What do I do?'

'You just go up and say, "Excuse me does Mrs Something live here?"'

'All right.' Cissie had gone pink again. 'I'll do it. I'll ask if Mrs Comberbach lives here. Nobody's ever called Comberbach.'

Up we trooped, knocked and waited for the nice, bored, wispy woman to answer, ready to stand and chat a minute and improve her afternoon. We pushed Cissie to the front, when we heard rather firm feet approaching. There's always a sort of agonized feeling before they answer.

'Does Mrs Com –' she started.

'– berbach live here?' she ended faintly; because the woman was not wispy at all. She was gigantic with large bones in her face, wearing a hat as if she'd just got in, but already bound round with aprons and holding a tin of Brasso. There was a smell of boiling floorcloths in the background.

'And if she does,' she said.

'Um – well. We 'eard she did,' said Cissie.

'You'd best come in then,' she said, 'if it's Mrs Comberbach you want to see.'

'Oh my crikeys!' said Florence.

Now I know this sort of woman. There are a lot of them round these parts – great long arms and legs and silent and knowing exactly what they're up to. Nothing Danish about them. They are part of the Old Norse Brigade, my father says, whatever that means, and they must be marvellous if you need rescuing from a burning building or something. But they are not exactly chatty or full of charms.

'Inside,' she said, stepping back, and you couldn't disagree. 'Tek off your shoes.' We took them off. It was one of those horrible halls where the lino's polished till it looks wet. We tiptoed over it into a fearfully clean front room with the coals arranged on the sticks like a jigsaw and the arm-chairs made out of brown skin and never sat on, and a terrified-looking plant standing eyes right in the window, wishing it were dead.

We all sat down on the upright chairs round the wall and Mrs Comberbach stood just inside the door watching us. She had put down the Brasso and folded her arms. Slowly she began to scratch her elbows. We sat there while the pointers of the electric clock went silently and swiftly and agonizingly on.

'Well, let's hear what it is, then,' she said at last, and Florence started about being on the way back from dinner or something, but got no further than three words.

'Let's hear what it's about,' she repeated. 'You stays here until. I wasn't born yesterday.'

So we had the most terrible quarter of an hour, as she didn't seem to have any understanding at all, just kept on asking silly questions and glaring. 'Going into houses,' she said. 'To think that daft game's still going. I wasn't born yesterday.' Then she vanished into the kitchen among the floorcloths and she'd got us into such a state that we just went on sitting there, not stirring. It was ages before we started wondering if we could get to our shoes and make a dash for it and Florence and I had just got up to try when in she marched again with a great tray.

'Brambles and sugar,' she said. 'It's a treat,' and she stood watching us without blinking. 'Watch the wallpaper. And your clothes,' she added. 'And eat up. I want four clean plates.'

'An 'orrible cow,' Cissie said outside in The Cut about a million years later. And wrong as usual because the woman hadn't done anything bad or unkind – kind in fact in her own way.

(*NOTE*

You will think me fairly stupid but it was only the other day that I realized that this woman probably wasn't called Mrs Comberbach at all. I didn't let on to the others, as a matter of fact, that I ever *had* thought so, or only to Florence anyway. She said, 'Good lord, if you believed that you would believe anything.' But she isn't interested in coincidence, Florence, being good at Mathematics, though my father says she will become more interested in it after L.C.M.s.

When I asked my father if it *could* have been Mrs Comberbach, he said it could. When you definitely prove otherwise he said, THE GAME IS UP.)

*

'I have no alternative,' said Miss Dobbs as we stood in the front in a row, 'since you are TWENTY-FIVE minutes late and the lesson nearly over but to give you an order mark – all of you. Yes, well – I'm sorry but in fact I am being extremely lenient – more lenient than I have any right to be. It is simply because most of you are very good girls – most of you – and I feel that you must have been in*cited* into this business in some way.' She stopped for a long hard look, but we were looking downwards. 'What on earth were you doing? Florence Bone of all people! Helen Bell! Being led off to visit Cissie's relations. And down The Cut! You know The Cut is out of bounds. You must know that you have to keep to the definite route Laid Down. If there were an air raid, how should we know where to find you if you were allowed to roam all over the town? This is a Very Serious Matter. Go and sit down all of you. I shall have to think about whether it must be Reported.'

She breathed heavily once or twice. She is a fine-looking woman, Miss Dobbs, with a noble sort of figure and a great deal of golden hair. Some of it is on her chin. On the hockey field she cries 'Up the FIIIIIIELD, Forwards,' and she looks just like a Viking.

'And now,' she said, 'I am afraid we must leave *The Cloister and the Hearth* and turn to your essays of last week-end. I am going to tell you right away that there was one essay that was much better than any of the others and it was an even pleasanter surprise to see it because it was by somebody quite unexpected – someone I had never guessed could describe things so well. A really lovely essay, and I want it back please because I want to show it to the Headmistress and see if she will include part of it in the school magazine. Here you are then – Dorothy Hobson. A really good effort. Ten out of ten.

'Now then.' She began to give the books back one by one, sometimes stabbing with her pencil here and there as she pointed something out. The pile grew smaller until there was only one book left.

'And now, Jessica. Will you come here please? Jessica, what was the meaning of this? I have kept yours to the end. What *was* the meaning of it ?'

I lifted one of my feet a little way from the floor and at the same time I wondered why people do stand on one leg at moments like this. Horses lift up a foot when they're ready to kick and dogs when they're ready to run. I wasn't thinking of doing either. Everyone was watching. I examined carefully the little wheels on the bottom of her desk and I began to smile because I didn't know what to say and my eyes had gone hot.

'The title of this essay, Jessica, was "The Best Day of the Summer Holidays", wasn't it?'

'Yes, Miss Dobbs.'

'Then may I ask, Jessica, why you felt you had to write forty-seven pages?'

'Well, I just wanted to.'

'But you see, it wasn't on the subject. In the first place it was about something that happened before the holidays started – the day you broke up in fact, not in the holidays at all. And in the second place it was so *pointless*, so *silly*. All about some woman in a tea-shop, some woman you had obviously MADE UP, a sort of witch. Now I've no objection to you using your imagination and inventing characters, that is splendid, but you must not try to pass people off as real who never existed when you are asked for FACTS. FACTS, Jessica. It isn't even as if you were telling a story – you were trying to make a story where there was no story. It was an ESSAY I asked for. I'm afraid what you gave me looked awfully like a *lie*.'

I didn't say a thing.

'And –' she shoved her bottom about her seat, 'and it was all so *shapeless*, Jessica. Look, let's treat it as a story for a moment, shall we? A story must have a beginning and a middle and an end – as of course an essay must, too. So look – look here. This could come out, and this and this.' The red pencil went slashing through chunk after chunk. 'And you see, Jessica, it was all so – well all so pleased with itself somehow. So self-conscious. When you have finished anything, you know, you should read it through and – listen now, listen all of you. I'm going to give you a very good rule that was given to me at college and I have always been abundantly grateful for it. When you have written something that you think is really good, destroy it. Destroy it.

'Dear,' she added. 'Throw it right away. If you don't you will feel terribly ashamed of it afterwards.

'Do you see, dear?' I could feel that she was looking more closely at the top of my head, and there was a sort of kindness beginning to be in the air. 'It must have taken you such a long time, dear. I don't expect you to spend so much of your weekend – and after all you have very little time when it comes to The Exams. It must have quite spoiled your Saturday.'

'I ADORED IT!' Up came my face. 'I adored it, you cuckoo!'

I picked up *The Cloister and the Hearth* from her desk. 'And if mine's long what about his? It's an awful long book and it's dead boring and *he* was jolly pleased with himself if anyone was. He's no good, the rambly old thing. If I'd written a lousy book like that I *would* have destroyed it. I *would* have burned it up. All that romantic tosh about monks. You don't need to go writing about that sort of make-up tosh . . .'

'Be quiet!'

'. . . there's plenty going on all the time. And it was true, my story – my essay. You're a fool.'

'Take an order mark,' she squealed. 'Leave the room. Go and sit in the shoe-bags. Go out. Go!'

'It's a lousy, sloppy, rambling, boring book. Why can't we read some good books? Why can't we read some plays? Why can't we read some poetry? I am a writer beyond all possible . . .'

But she'd got me by the middle of the back of my gym-slip and was carrying me through the air out of sight. And I fell in the shoe-bags and burst into tears.

4

G oodness knows how long I cried but after what seemed ages I realized that I was making a terrible noise. I listened to myself. When you reach this stage the first part of misery is over. Then it all comes back, with more memory in it, and off you go again much worse than before. I sobbed and sobbed. Apart from me there was absolute silence in the cloakrooms and all the coats and hats and bags hung uselessly round about me in lumps.

Then the back door of the school opened and feet came by, passing quite close to me, flip-flap, flip-flap, flip-flap, flip. They faded off and I heard the great front door on to the sea-front open and slam behind someone. Then I heard it open again and the feet return, flip-flap, flip-flap, flip-flap, flip. I looked out of the folds of the shoe bags and saw a grey-haired, very small woman with her petticoat coming down. Her face had a very wide smile on it and her head swung up and down. She was wearing a navy blue felt hat with a curiously uneven brim and carrying a huge, battered suitcase which, as she stood there, burst open and spilled exercise books all over the floor.

'There now!' she said. 'Thank goodness I came back. They'd have gone all over the esplanade and down among the mines on the beach. I wonder if those people in the gun-emplacements would have allowed me to go over the barbed-wire to get them back? Is something the matter, dear? Aren't you well?'

'I've had an order mark.'

'Oh dear, I'm sorry. But if it was just one . . .'

'It was three.'

'Three!'

'Yes. Three in a day.'

'Oh my word!'

'And it wasn't my fault.'

'But how dreadful!'

'Absolutely, utterly not my fault,' and sob, wail, howl, I started again, sort of angrily now, too.

'You are blaring,' said the woman sitting down on a locker. (I knew who it was. It was old Miss Philemon, the Senior English mistress. Everybody knew her – she was famous and had written books. She had been to Oxford in the days when the only girls who went to Oxford were those who could take their mothers and aunts with them to take care of them, they were so old-fashioned. I had seen her once or twice before taking a short cut through the Junior School from her flat further along the sea-front on her way up to teach the Seniors.) 'Stop blaring, dear,' she said. 'I wish I had a handkerchief for you but I seem to have . . . oh thank you dear, that's right. All in again, I do get so behind with my marking. Blaring is a lovely word isn't it? And still used you know in the northwest to describe the noise made by miserable and disturbed cows. A Saxon word perhaps? The Saxons used wonderful words to describe what they really knew about, like God and the sea and cattle. There are wonderful Viking words, too, but the Vikings couldn't touch the Saxons for poetry. They were terribly busy, healthy sort of men, the Vikings, always out of doors and shouting. I suppose one shouldn't say it since they're on our side, but the Vikings rather remind me of *Americans*. While the Saxons — there's no getting away from it — are Germans. Now tell me about the order marks.'

I said that they all thought I was above myself and I ought to be set down and that someone had heard them saying so in the staffroom.

'Oh dear! How old are you about?'

'Twelve.'

'Oh, you poor thing! Are you indeed? I really hated twelve — *and* thirteen. And then somebody told me that it was all to do with growing. It was all to do with my inside. With my *stomach* I believe in some way. I was so relieved. I had thought I was growing unpleasant and starting to hate everyone, and I didn't want to be that sort of person at all. It all calmed down later on. I do remember though that I spent a lot of time crying. But childhood is such a wretched time anyway. Have you noticed in the street, or in a bus or anywhere, if you stop and listen you can nearly always hear a child crying? It's perfectly awful when you come to think of it. If we were to be quiet now . . .' ('Gulp, gulp') 'Well, there you are. Exactly! At the moment poor girl, it is you. It is in the *stomach*, dear.'

'That's nothing to do with it!' I was in a rage and I glared at her. 'It isn't my stomach. It's my essay. It's a good essay. I know it's a good essay. She said it was awful and I was too pleased with myself. She said it was a lie. I called her a fool.'

'It was not right to call her a fool.'

'Yes, well I'm sorry. No I'm not. She is a fool.'

'We are all fools.' She nodded and smiled.

'She said I ought to have burnt it up. Because I liked it. She made it sound like a sin or something. She said it must have spoiled my weekend . . .' Miss Philemon's face went all hazy and I couldn't stop my mouth ends going down.

'What a pity,' said Miss Philemon, smiling away. 'But if it was good, dear, that's all that matters. Perhaps she made a mistake. People do make mistakes. Think of the poor critics who laughed at Keats and Wordsworth and Coleridge. Such idiots they look now.'

I said I didn't think the essay was *that* good. I hadn't been saying that. All I'd been saying was . . .

'It doesn't do writers much harm to suffer, you know,' she said. 'Usually it is praise that does them the harm. Though there was poor John Clare – one doesn't like to think of that. But even he had great compensations. Oh great compensations. He watched the glory of God, you know.' She said this in an ordinary way. 'And then there was Chatterton – but you know I never believed all that about a broken heart. Usually if a poet's good he doesn't break his heart. Can you imagine Emily Brontë crumpling up with a broken heart? No, of course you can't. She'd start working instead. Like Keats who said when he was really in despair

45

he put a clean shirt on. Though mind you he was very lucky, being a man he wouldn't have had to wash it and iron it himself first . . .'

She went on and on and on about people I hadn't heard of. At last she asked again, 'Tell me about the order marks.'

'Well, the first one was for refusing to eat worms. And there were worms. All over the plate,' and I looked blazingly at her so that she would see this thing about me, that I can't help telling the truth. 'There were purple worms all over the brambles, full of juice. I couldn't eat them.'

'No indeed.' She shut her eyes for a moment.

'And then there was this thing about Cissie Comberbach.'

'Cissie Comberbach! *Is* there anybody called Cissie Comberbach?'

'There are two.' And I told her.

'NO!' said Miss Philemon.

'Yes,' I said. 'Really. At least I think so. It was a bit funny.' I told her about the brambles.

She began to laugh. It was a queer, high, frail sound like someone calling far away across a meadow. Higher and higher it went and her eyes began to stream and her hair began to come down and her hat fell off. 'Hoo, hoo, hoo,' she wept and I found I was joining in. We laughed and laughed and laughed and laughed, and in the middle Miss Dobbs came flying out of the classroom.

'JESSICA VYE!' she roared. 'What is it now? What are you doing? Who is it you've got there in the shoe-bags?'

'It's me,' said Miss Philemon, 'or I suppose I should say "It is I", only no one ever does. Sometime soon the dictionary will have to be changed. Marjorie dear, I'm sorry. Did I disturb your lesson? This child – she is wanting to apologize to you, by the way, go along . . .'

'I'm sorry,' I said.

'That's right. This girl has told me one of the oddest things I've ever heard. Oh, such a thing and a ridiculous thing. Get her to tell you it, dear. It will cheer you up.'

She put on her hat and picked up her suitcase and went flip-flap over to the door. Miss Dobbs said never a word.

'Goodbye, dears,' she said, and opened the great front door on to a huge orange sky over the steelworks beyond the estuary. She looked up at it like a shepherd. 'I wouldn't wonder if we had a raid tonight,' she said. Then as she set forth with her big bag she said, 'Order marks!'

'Order marks!' she said. 'What nonsense!'

5

Time passed quite gently on for a week after this. Everyone rather ignored me. Miss Dobbs ignored me utterly and nobody said a single thing about the scene I'd made or asked what all the noise had been in the shoe-bags. Miss Birdwood seemed a bit uneasy when she caught my eye once in dinner, and we didn't have brambles again, but things were I should say if anything rather better. I wasn't exactly popular of course but I seemed to be feeling different about it. I dug into my desk lid very deep during Hygiene with my compass's end and filled up the holes with ink and saw I'd written John Clare. Underneath it I wrote The Glory of God even deeper still. I expect it will be there for generations. When Helen saw it she turned away looking as if she would be sick.

Then one day Cissie came worming up and said, 'You're going to the Head.' It was in dinner and she was the server over on the big girls' table and she had heard them talking. 'What?' I said. I thought I'd heard wrong because she has this awful posh cockney voice which makes her difficult to understand – 'laaaaas night' and so on: also she was making even more than her usual noise with her knife and fork because you have to eat fast when you're a server to be in time for clearing. 'I don't care,' I said.

'Not likely!' ('No' loikly!')

Florence said, 'Oh shut up. You're inventing it.'

'No I aren't. I 'eard that big prefect asking who Jessica Vye was because she was in trouble and was going to be Sent For. She said she was outside the staffroom door. The Head said it was a small matter but rather disturbing and Jessica Vye was obviously a ring-leader.'

I was very surprised at that. I just stared out of the window. I don't think anything could have surprised me as much as that. A '*ring*-leader'? Think of me with a ring! It couldn't be the essay-business anyway. No one could call that a ring. Absolutely nobody joined up with me over that. They'd all just sat there . . .

'What else did she hear?' asked Florence.

Something about putting children in concentration camps.'

'What!'

'She said one of the staff said, "Oh Headmistress, they don't have much fun. Surely she might be let off" and Miss LeBouche said, "Come come, Miss Macmillan. Aren't we being a little sentimental. Think of the children of Poland."'

'Crippen, Jessica, what *have* you been doing now?'

We went back to school.

I waited for something to happen but nothing did, nor the next day nor the next. I began to think it was just Cissie. Then on the Friday at the beginning of the first lesson in the afternoon, old Dobbs, without looking at me but just turning to the blackboard said, 'Oh, Jessica, will you go upstairs and see Miss Macmillan please,' and I got this terrible frightened feeling in my inside. Rather lower than my inside. Actually it was quite nice.

I knocked on the door upstairs and Miss Macmillan who is the head of the Junior School put her face out and said, 'Oh yes, Jessica. The Headmistress wants to see you. Will you go up to Big School now please?' So I went down again and got my gas mask and set off. As I closed the back door of the yard I looked up at Miss Macmillan's window and there she was looking out with a kind face. She dropped the curtain at once and moved back, but because of this gift I have I knew what she was thinking: 'Poor Jessica. She has Absolutely No Idea!' I have seen this look on people's faces before.

Off I went up Ginger Street again. I had come down it only a quarter of an hour before, back from dinner, and it did seem silly that they couldn't have told me while I was up there because as I've said before the Headmistress's house was just across the road from the Senior School. In fact it seemed to me that I might have gone in to see her in her sitting-room while she was eating her dinner. It would have saved everyone a lot of time and it would have been friendlier.

However, I was only missing English and it made a change. I was really quite interested to meet Miss LeBouche. She kept herself so pale and far. She was so unreal, standing on the platform every term end, saying 'God be in my head', so far away. I tried to think of the exact word for her and could only think 'papery'. 'Papery-pale,' I said. But it wasn't quite right. I began to feel rather excited.

When I got to the school I found I didn't know how to get into it. Although I'd passed the big main gates with the steps going straight up behind them twice a day for over a year I had never actually seen anyone going through them. At the beginning of term we always went in a crocodile somewhere round the back. The big doors at the top of the steps had the look of a sort of stage about them, well-painted with a shiny brass plate. They were shut. I made my way round to the back instead and got lost among some dustbins. I tried again and found myself in the air-raid shelters. Then I had another go and got into a big quadrangle with quiet formrooms all round it. Here and there in the windows you could see the top halves of teachers standing, talking to the air and waving chalk about. You couldn't see any girls because they were all sitting down. It looked very funny and I stood all alone in the sunshine grinning like mad.

A big girl came along after a while along the cloisters towards the W.C.s and looked at me curiously. 'What's the matter with you?' she asked.

'I've got to go and see Miss LeBouche.'

She looked sorry for me. 'It's through here, turn right, then turn left and you're in the Hall. There's a door on the other side of the Hall with "Silence" on it and a chair. You just sit on the chair.'

I did all this.

I looked round the Hall which was also the gym. All the

queer bits of furniture you flung yourself about on were put away neatly. The long ropes were looped back like curtains and the October sun came streaming down from the high windows near the roof on to the most enormous, golden, empty floor. Looking at it made me happy. Next year I'd be here, playing here, climbing the ropes. I could climb ropes. I had learned when I was seven in our old garden. We'd had a rope in a sycamore tree. 'They'll be surprised at *that*,' I thought, and fell asleep.

I woke up to a great strumming on a piano and a noise of thunder, 'ONE, TWO,' a great voice calling, and Boom, Boom. Some gigantic girls went hurtling over a great leather headless animal with handles sticking out of its back. It was standing right in front of me. 'Troy,' I thought, 'no – air-raid.' There had been an air-raid the night before. We had been in the shelter until six o'clock and my mother had been nearly hit by a bit of shrapnel in the yard. In fact she had been hit but she'd had her tin hat on. 'Just look at this!' she had said in disgust, coming back into the shelter, holding out the shrapnel, 'Right on my hat!' 'You make it sound like bird droppings,' my father had said. It's funny how you forget air-raids in the day. I thought of them laughing and looking at the shrapnel, and Ma's disgusted face, and I smiled too and looked up into the face of a very serious, cool person in gold-edged glasses. 'Hello,' I said. Then I remembered!

I shot to my feet.

'Come in,' said Miss LeBouche. 'How long have you been sitting there?'

'I don't know Miss LeBouche,' I added.

'Did you knock?'

'No.' (Why hadn't I thought of knocking? Florence would have. They probably all would have. I began to feel confused about myself, not being quite awake.)

'Really? This is rather odd, isn't it?'

I couldn't think of a thing to say. But I suddenly realized that although I was feeling confused I was also feeling nice after the sleep in the sun: so I smiled at her. I saw her think, 'She has a pleasant face. Teeth too big but they often are at that age. Good cheekbones. Hardly a trace of an accent. Odd. She looks an artless little thing.'

'I believe, Jessica,' she said, 'that you were given three order marks in one day at the beginning of term.'

So it was that. Oh well. 'Yes, Miss LeBouche.'

'Can you give me an explanation?'

'Oh yes,' I said. I was pleased it was starting like this. 'Yes I can. As a matter of fact I'd be very glad to. I've already talked and talked about it to Miss Philemon. It was a perfectly dreadful day – dreadful from beginning to end. It almost makes you believe in bewitchments – like the milk going sour and so on and being careful not to do things at the full moon. Like Puck or something. Please can I tell you about it because it was awful, but, I don't know why, even though it was awful I'm very glad it happened because something terribly funny came out of it. I told Miss Philemon and she laughed and laughed in the shoe-bags. She actually held the shoe-bags to her face. She told me it was the oddest thing she'd ever heard. She told me a great many things, such as that two old ladies were walking along a street one day and they saw a man sitting in a bow window on a promenade with a pen in his hand and he was laughing and laughing and the tears running, laughing at WHAT HE HAD WRITTEN. She said it was better to be like him than like a lot of people. She said that there is absolutely no harm in trying to be funny. She said that John Clare had turned out the winner in spite of what they did to him and that he had seen the Glory of God . . .'

'ONE MOMENT!'

'The man laughing,' I said (since nothing happened for ages), 'was Dickens.'

'STOP!'

'Yes, Miss LeBouche.'

'Can you tell me whether or not it is true that you and some friends were eating large bags of potato-chips on the train at five o'clock one evening last term?'

'Yes, Miss LeBouche.'

'You look bewildered. Did it not occur to you that this was a somewhat disagreeable thing to do?'

'No.' I looked at her.

'I see.' (She was thinking, 'This child is simple.') 'Well, I am sorry to say that it strikes me as being so. It also struck the station-master and the ladies in the ticket office. They say that you were *mouthing* at one another, and throwing chips about.'

'We were not doing that,' I said very decidedly. 'We'd never have thrown any away. They were lovely. We may have waved them about a bit or waggled them . . .'

'STOP!" she cried again.

'Miss LeBouche, I know we weren't mouthing or throwing chips. He's an awful old man and his trousers are always undone and he hates . . .'

'STOP, STOP!'

I stopped and she breathed slowly for a time. 'Jessica,' she said, 'you are very fluent, and I am wondering if you are the sort of girl to whom punishment means very much.'

'But I haven't done anything. I mean *punishment* . . . !'

'Will you be quiet! Can I ask you one question. From the way you speak, the construction of your sentences, I can see that you are a lady. Can you promise me that in future you will try to remember that? That you will try to behave with decorum. You are – let me see – nearly thirteen years old. It is time to start thinking of such things as reticence; a little less emotion. Will you promise me to try to behave like a gentlewoman?'

I was silent and then I said, 'I'm terribly sorry but I'm afraid I can't.'

'And why not?'

'Well, I'm not one. I'm not a gentlewoman.'

'Oh?'

'I will try to be good, I really will. As a matter of fact I do. I think that's another reason I'm so unpopular, but you really have to in our house, it's part of father's job. But I can't be a gentlewoman because father doesn't believe in it. He's a member of the Labour Party.'

She said, '*I* see,' and looked at her finger nails. 'Well, never mind. Shall we leave it at that then, that you will *try* to be good? That is really what I meant. You know it all comes down to goodness in the end, as you will see if you read about Our Lord. Now I wonder if you have anything to say?'

I thought for ages and said that I should like to ask please the meaning of 'decorum' because it was a word I didn't know, and for the first time she nearly hit the ceiling. 'Dignity,' she thundered, 'dignity, child, dignity,' louder, I think, than she had meant . . .

'And please . . .' (I'd obviously not said the right thing.)

'Yes? I'm very busy.' (Because of this gift I have I saw what she was thinking: 'The child is not simple at all, she is *knowing*. She is a nasty child, a nasty knowing child . . .')

'Please, Miss LeBouche, I'm not actually sure that Our Lord *was* particularly good in the way you mean. My father thinks He must have been rebellious and difficult . . . And actually honestly I can't see why we can't eat chips when term's actually over.'

She gave me a conduct mark. Even though I'd got to the door and was fiddling with the little keyhole cover thing below the knob. I had been nearly out in fact. Thank goodness she didn't seem to have caught on that if you got three order marks you got a conduct mark automatically and that this was therefore really my second conduct mark which meant I was expelled. Cissie had said so anyway, though goodness knows how she knew. Nobody had ever really known anyone who had *had* three order marks in one day, and then a conduct mark, so it was all guesswork.

But they'd have to have a meeting about it first you'd

think. They'd surely write to your parents? Perhaps Miss LeBouche was, of course. Perhaps she was writing to my parents this very minute. Or perhaps she hadn't realized yet that she had a right to expel me. Perhaps I really ought to go back and tell her. After all I had promised to be good. I must behave as Our Lord would have behaved and I gave very careful thought to this. But I decided quite honestly that He wouldn't have gone back. This was a relief.

'I can't help the way I talk,' I thought, 'I really can't. My father's the same after all. It's inherited. But it's all right for him, he's allowed. Teachers and parsons and actors and dictators and prime ministers . . . If I wasn't a writer beyond all possible doubt perhaps the thing to be would be an actress.' And I saw myself suddenly upon a stage, dressed in black from head to foot, so sharp and definite it was like a vision. I was holding a dagger and light flashed outside brightening a stained-glass window at the back like Elsie Meeney's. A turret room in a lonely wood. Yet if it were a stained-glass window you wouldn't be able to see the trees. I pondered how they would do it. I had not been to a theatre but I had seen *Rebecca* on the pictures and *Marie Walewska* and *The Scarlet Pimpernel* with Leslie Howard. We'd done *Midsummer Night's Dream* in class which is a poor play but for some reason however awfully you read it and even with Cissie Comberbach as Peaseblossom you somehow keep thinking of it and the peasant bits in the wood do come out terribly funny especially if you give Bottom a very high voice in the Pyramus bits, you can make them die laughing and even old Dobbs smile. And the wood, if you had a stage, could probably be made to look marvellous if you got some green . . . Good heavens!

I was walking through a wood. I stopped and looked all round. It was quite a thick wood growing all down the side of a bank, trees above me, trees below. I was on a narrow waving path. All under the trees, up and down in all directions a plant was growing with heavy, curved-back leaves and lacy white flowers. There was a strong smell of onions. 'Garlic,' I thought, 'I must be in the sea-wood. How on earth did I get here?'

Once or twice a year the Juniors are taken to the sea-wood for Nature. There is a stream at the bottom that rattles along to the sea except when the tide is high and pushes the stream back. The stream is red coming down from the moors because of the ironstone, but foaming and greenish and salty when it is being pushed back again. At the foot of the wood where the stream runs, the ground flattens out fairly wide for a stretch and green grass grows there. The Town Council long ago planted gardens on this stretch, when Cleveland Spa was a fashionable place, more genteel than Scarborough, where ladies came with parasols and great families of children with nursemaids and sailor suits and hoops. There is a little bandstand down there and ornamental flower-beds called the Valley Gardens. After leaving Miss LeBouche I must have wandered towards the sea-wood on the road going round the back of the school instead of on to the ordinary main road towards Ginger Street. How on earth had I done that?

'I must be half asleep,' I thought. 'It must be being up last night or something. Crikey! They'll kill me if they find me. They nearly went mad when I only went down The Cut. Oh heavens, I didn't mean to come this way, honestly I didn't. Honestly!' I began to run.

I ran until the bandstand came in sight beneath me and then I stopped for breath. The sun shone on the little white bandstand. It looked like a doily for a cake, all lace, standing in the green valley, surrounded by diamond-shaped beds of dahlias, great splashes of scarlet and yellow and blood-red and orange. There had been no gardeners for the Valley Gardens since the war began, but it was a sheltered place and I suppose the frost had kept away. The dahlias were bloom-ing and blazing like warriors, though they can't have even been touched through the winter. The gold sunshine shone in level rays – oh heavens! it must be just about the end of the afternoon! – into the bandstand, and inside the band-stand, lying on his back across three metal chairs was a man dressed in a blue battle-dress, quite still.

I forgot everything that had happened then that afternoon. I forgot myself, my thoughts, my feelings, my fears. I was filled with a sort of sudden overpowering joy and love. The white, lacy little building, the blue man, the scarlet flowers, the heavy golden light, the banks of curly thick dark leaves under the autumn trees, the sound of the water and the salt in the air; and I just sat down in the garlic and gazed.

All of a sudden the man got up and walked across to one of the posts of the bandstand and embraced it. Then embrac-ing it he began to kick it. Then, more surprising still, and I sat up straight, he walked over to the nearest flower-bed and began to tear at the dahlias. He heaved and tugged and snarled at them. He began to fling them about and smear them into the ground under his feet. Then he brought a knife out of his pocket and began to slash at them in a frenzy, shouting at them, and roaring.

'STOP IT!" I was on my feet and running. 'Stop it, this minute. Do you hear me?' He stopped. 'Give me that knife.' He looked down at the knife in his hands with surprise and put it away in his pocket. 'How could you!' I yelled. I had tears in my eyes and I was absolutely shaking with rage. 'How could you! How could you! How could you! They're beautiful, you pig! You pig! They're beautiful.'

The man sat down on the grass and began to cry.

'Cry away,' I said. 'Cry away. How could you!' I pointed at the mess of flowers, the trampled bed, 'Oh you dreadful, dreadful man!' His black, curly head turned this way and that on his brown arms and sobs heaved him about on the green grass. 'Oh shut up,' I said, but he went on.

'Shut up,' I said after a bit, 'it's all right. Don't cry.' His hair started at a dot in the middle and went round and round in curls and I stretched out my hand and touched it. Then I patted his head.

He stopped crying and looked up and his face was thoroughly wet. I saw him looking at my awful navy gym-slip and square-necked grey shirt and my face which must have been very fierce, and a look came into his eyes that I had absolutely never seen before, or not in faces looking at me. It was a liking-sort of look but a queer liking-look. It was sort of excited, as if he had found something.

I suddenly felt very cold and at the same moment the sun went off the Valley Gardens and we were in the shadows. 'I must be going now,' I said, and with very great Dignity and Decorum I marched away. Steady and straight I went, up through the gardens, up through the garlic, up into the little wavy path in the trees. I couldn't look round. The whole of my back from heels to my head was cold and prickling.

'Hey!' came from down below. 'Hey! Come back. You very preety,' and I ran. I ran and ran. The trees dropped behind and on and on I ran and I heard a crackling sound behind and thudding feet, heavy and hard, and I cried, 'Oh God! Oh God, help me! Oh God!' and I burst out of the gateway of the sea-wood with its two stone columns and pompous steps and the wide, empty promenade above them, hardly a hundred yards from the Junior School and safety.

I burst through the door in the school yard at the back into the middle of all the train girls lining up for home.

'Jessica!' said Miss Macmillan, 'I say, you have been a long time! Get in line now, you're just in time for the train.'

'Whatshesay?' asked Dottie Hobson.

'Who? What?'

'Miss LeB?'

'Oh her – oh I don't know. Something. I got a conduct mark.

'Gosh, how awful!'

'Why you puffing?' asked Florence.

'Been running.'

'Why didn't you go straight to the station?'

'Don't know.'

'She did keep you ages. Poor old you. I say, we're having two Staff to take us to the station today. A poor old Eye-tie prisoner's escaped.'

'What's an Eye-tie prisoner?'

'Oh Jessica! An *Italian* – one of the prisoners working on the farms. He ran off this morning and they couldn't find him.'

'Come along, line up,' said Miss Macmillan.

'They say he's *armed*,' whispered Helen. 'He's *terribly* dangerous. He's a maniac.'

'Nonsense,' said Miss Macmillan, overhearing. 'He's probably just miserable and longing for home. Still – better keep out of his way all of you.'

'Oh my word,' I thought. 'Oh my crikeys! Oh heavens!'

All the way home, all through tea, all through homework I tried to feel afraid, but I couldn't. Not afraid and wicked as I knew I was supposed to do. On and on in bed I thought about it. On and on about his hair and his wet face and the look in his eyes. 'You very preety,' he had said. Oh heavens, how awful! But oh heavens, how lovely, too!

6

I caught the quarter to eight train to school the next morning, saying I was flower monitress or something – which I was – and went left under the subway to Miss Philemon's flat. I had to beat my way against the wind and rain along the promenade as I had forgotten my macintosh. It was a foul dark morning. You couldn't have believed in the sun of yesterday afternoon. I climbed the four flights up to the flat and rang the bell, and she came to the door eating Marie biscuits.

'Come in,' she said, 'my goodness me, you're wet!' She stood back blinking and smiling. There was a great sniff over by the window and Miss Crake, the art mistress, launched herself off the curtains and shambled across the room and out of the door behind me. She gave me the fright of my life. She was a huge-boned, bleak sort of woman who cared for nobody except Iris Ingledew who was the only girl in the school who could paint. She trailed a big carrier made of linoleum with paint-brushes sticking out of the top. What put me off was that she must have been watching me as I came along the sea-front. I wondered what she'd been saying.

'Sit down by the electric fire,' said Miss Philemon, 'and have a biscuit. I always have biscuits for breakfast – when I can get them that is. I do wish we could use our clothing coupons for food, don't you? I'd so much rather have food than clothing.'

I said, 'Yes,' and sat down and gazed at the electric fire, an awful old bent thing, and the clock started ticking very loudly.

'Miss Crake called in to tell me that they have caught the poor prisoner. Will you have some tea, dear? It hasn't been made long.' I said no thank you, and the clock ticked on. After a while Miss Philemon picked up her morning newspaper and began to read. I became stiller and stiller and suddenly I found I wasn't sitting there any more. At least I was. My body was but I was looking down at it from somewhere up near the ceiling. I saw the top of my head quite clearly, my hair dry in the middle where my school hat had been, and wet round the edges, and my feet stretched out to the fire. What a poor looking thing, I thought. It's grand to be free.

Then she rattled the paper and I returned with a jolt and a sigh. 'I think I'd better be going,' I said.

'That's right. You don't want to be late for prayers and neither do I.' I put on my horrible wet coat and hat and went down the stairs again and outside. But when I got on to the promenade I thought, 'I really ought to have told her why I came. She'll think I'm a bit funny. Anyone but her would have gone on and on to find out. It was really very good-mannered of her.'

I walked back upstairs to the flat's front door and rang again and Miss Philemon answered it, wearing her hat now and carrying the huge suitcase.

'I thought I'd better tell you what it was,' I said. 'When you said Miss Crake had heard they'd caught him I thought it would be all right. But still, I think I ought to tell you why I came.'

'Are you sure you must?' she said. 'Some things are much better kept to oneself. Don't feel you have to tell people everything. It is a great mistake. You often lose things if you pass them around. If you have been doing something wrong don't think you'll get rid of it by passing it to me.'

'No,' I said, 'it's nothing wrong. But I'd better tell you. It's about the prisoner. I met him.'

'You – what dear?'

'Met him. I met him yesterday afternoon in the sea-wood. He was bashing and bashing his head against the bandstand.'

Instead of saying 'Whatever were you doing in the sea-wood?' she said, 'Did he see you?'

'Well he wouldn't of.'

'"Would not have done",' she said.

'Would not have done. But he started smashing at the dahlias.'

'Smashing?'

'Well, slashing. Pulling them and slashing them with a knife, and swearing at them. So I went for him.'

Miss Philemon sat down suddenly on the nearest chair and shut her eyes. 'Yes?' she said.

'I went for him and said he mustn't spoil them and he

was horrible and shouted like anything, and then he started crying and sat down on the grass.'

She said, 'Go on.'

'And, then I felt sorry for him and – well I went away and left him there.'

She put down her case which she had forgotten to put down before and stood up and went over to the window and looked out through the rain at the cliffs. Her voice sounded different and I went all cold again like yesterday.

'Did this man touch you?'

'No.'

'Do you swear this?'

'Yes.'

'You do realize that you were in great danger.'

'Yes, Miss Philemon.'

'Do you swear that you will never, never, never wander about in lonely places like this again? That if ever you find that you are alone with somebody behaving in this odd way you will go at once, that instant? That you will report it to the police?'

I didn't say anything.

'Do you swear this, Jessica? Otherwise I must tell Miss LeBouche. If the man had not been caught I should have had to tell her this minute. Do you swear that he didn't touch you?'

'Yes, Miss Philemon. Actually, I did touch him.'

'What!'

'I patted him. He was crying. He really was absolutely miserable. I don't think he would have hurt me.'

'You *patted* him?'

'Yes. I patted him on the head.'

'And then . . .?'

'And then I went away.'

'And if it happened again?'

I thought.

'It wouldn't,' I said. 'It won't. You see it was very . . . Well the sun was out, and there was this bandstand and the dahlias. And he was bashing and slashing and he was saying horrible words like an animal, a pig, a pig . . .' I was crying, and she said, 'Hush, let me think. Have a biscuit,' and the room went silent again except for the awful clanking tick of the alarm-clock. After ages she turned from the window and shook herself. '*All* right,' she said. 'All right. No more. We shall say no more. Not you and not I. Keep it and don't worry. Only promise me to take care. Promise me that you have learned something.'

I said, 'Yes, yes I do promise that.' (Though goodness knows what, I thought. Why can't she say a bit more? I began to feel fed up. She was being like other people now, hinting things and saying nothing.)

'So long,' she said, 'as you have told me everything?' I thought, 'Why haven't I? Why haven't I told her what he said? "You very preety." I bet no one ever told her that.'

'Off you go then. Off you go, child, before you miss prayers. You look tired. Don't worry any more.'

As I stood up I saw a picture over the mantelpiece of some women standing side by side carrying baskets of fruit. One had her head turned and was speaking quietly to the other.

They had no clothes on above their skirts and they were some sort of Africans. They were very steady and still against dark green trees. You could tell it was a man who was painting them and they were not easy about it. I couldn't look more than a blink and I fell over my feet and dashed out of the flat and down the stairs and along by the sea in the beastly rain with the wind pushing me along behind. I rushed through the shoe-bags and was just in time to line up for prayers.

'Very nice.'

'I said "Very nice" dear. Your essay. A very nice little essay.'

I went and got it and saw 'V.G. Excellent work' at the bottom in Dobbs's clear big writing. I slapped the book down on my desk and wound my legs round my chair again. Out of the window the long waves were rolling in blotted out now and again by the splatters of rain on the glass. They say there is no land between Cleveland Spa and the North Pole. My desk with John Clare on it, and the window frame and the road and the barbed wire are the last solid things until the ice begins. Far away out there are a few dismal penguins looking towards Cleveland Spa and some loping old bears waving their heads about. Nothing else breathing above the water. The wind battered and screamed.

'. . . be the first of many,' she was saying, '. . . lucid, . . . fluent . . . For you *have* ability, Jessica. And I am really quite impressed with your spelling and punctuation, though the actual hand-writing is very wild. Very interesting use of the semi-colon. Are you listening?'

'I'm sorry, Miss Dobbs.'

'I said I hope it will be the first of many.'

'Oh yes. Yes I can always do that sort of thing.'

'Oh you can, can you?' She began to push her books about and shift in her chair, and because of this gift I have I knew she was saying, 'Why do I dislike this child so much?' 'Jessie-Carr,' she said, 'will you please stop staring out of the window. You can read first today. Come along, *The Cloister and the Hearth*, Chapter ninety wasn't it?'

At Break we couldn't go out and had to cram into the hall – the big room at the front of the building where we had prayers. It had a piano in it and a splintery floor. The little girls in the first year pinged and ponged at the piano and pushed each other off the stool. There was a dismal sort of fire and the big girls huddled round it. I couldn't be bothered to push in although I was frozen and I went over to the window and stood staring at the sea again. After a while I began to roll the blackout cord all over my face.

'Why weren't you on the train, Jessie-Carr?'

'Oh shurrup.'

'Oh all right.' Helen flounced off. 'Antediluvian,' she said.

'What?'

'Oh nothing.'

'What's antediluvian when it's at home?'

'You are.'

'Good, I like being.'

'She doesn't know what it means,' said Florence. 'Don't worry, she probably made it up.'

'Jessica is so *fluent*. Jessie-Carr is so fluent,' said Dottie.

I rolled the blind cord and leaned my face on the window and Florence asked a question, which she hardly ever does in case she is intruding. 'What's the matter? What you thinking about?'

I said, 'Chocolate biscuits. Chocolate biscuits, cold ham, banana split, treacle tart. That woman in Elsie Meeney's. Eclairs. I'm ravenous.'

'What did you have for breakfast?'

'Can't remember. It was early. I had to get the early train.'

The little girls were squealing, '*When the war is OVER*' at the top of their beastly voices. Some of them had got a rope and were skipping on the bare boards. I said, 'Oh help! I've got a flaming headache.'

'Why did you get the early train?'

'Oh, I had to take something.'

'Take something?'

'Just to Miss Philemon's flat.' Florence said nothing and the little girls screamed, '*So cheery, cheery OH!*'

'I went in.'

'Did you? How . . .'

'Oh it's just a flat,' I said. 'Just a flat. But honestly! What a mess. Honestly, you've never seen! Mess everywhere. Books on the floor, under the sofa, on the mantelpiece. Her butter ration was on the clock. There's clothes all over the place and she was eating Marie biscuits. Old Crake was there too, and she was eating Marie biscuits. And all her brushes sticking out of that bag. Miss P. was in that hat with the brim waving about – I think she's trimmed it herself. She says she can't be bothered with clothes, and I said, 'You don't say!' Well I didn't but I nearly did.'

'I thought you liked Miss Philemon.'

'Liked her? What made you think I liked her? She's cracked. You ought to see the mess. Old tins lying around – sardines and stuff and old green bread – and her pictures! She's got filthy pictures.'

'What pictures?'

'Well one picture anyway. On the wall. Above the fireplace.'

'What was it?'

'Well, don't say anything but it was some women, green women, and they were *bare*.'

'What, all bare?'

'No, their top halfs.'

'Crippen, how big?'

'Enormous.'

'What were they doing?'

'Just standing about. Holding fruit. And all their bosoms!'

'Crikey! Have you told Dottie ?'

We went into lessons and it was Geography. Miss Pemberton said almost at once, 'That will do now. I don't mind a bit of talking when it's only tracing, but you are getting wild in that corner. What on earth is the matter, Helen?'

There were gulps and snorts and queer noises, especially from Dottie who asked if she could go for a drink of water and dropped a note on Betty Dawley's desk as she passed. It said, 'Miss Philemon has got a picture of green bosoms. Passiton.' Betty Dawley read it carefully, sniffed and passed it to Joan Pearson who read it with distaste. They raised their eyebrows and shoulders at each other and Betty yawned. 'Some people have got a funny sense of humour,' said Joan.

'Antediluvian,' said Betty.

'For goodness *sake*!' said Miss Pemberton. 'What is the row in the corner? It's like the Marx Brothers. Clatter, clatter, gulp and crash. You are a silly lot. Betty, what did you say just then?'

'Antediluvian,' said Betty going pink but looking as if she didn't care who knew it.

'*What* is antediluvian? Me, I suppose. Well I feel it this morning so I'll agree with you. Get on with the Rift Valley. That's even more so.' ('I told you antediluvian wasn't disgusting,' said Florence.)

'My Granny says "buzzums",' said Cissie and I began to snort like a pig. 'Nine green buzzums,' sang Florence in her booming whisper, 'Hanging on the wall. Nine green buzzums,

'If nine green buzzums
Should accidentally fall . . .'

'Right. I've had enough,' said Miss Pemberton. 'Bring me that piece of paper, Betty and let's see what it's all about.'

Betty stood up with a triumphant turn of her head and an air of being above it all. 'I don't know what it is,' she said. 'It was just put on my desk by someone.' She picked it up in her

finger tips and set off across the room with it, but fell over
on the way because of Florence's stretched-out foot and in
the scrabble to get it back only got half of it so that it read
'. . . picture of green bosoms'. Florence quickly swallowed
'Miss Philemon has a . . .'

'"Picture of green . . ." Good heavens, it looks like
BOSOMS.' Miss P. stared all round us. There were twenty-one
of us all gazing back at her – some blankly, some anxiously,
some (Cissie horrible Comberbach) with a creepy sort of
excitement. When she got to my face she kept on looking
and because of this gift I have I knew she was thinking how
plain we all were and me in particular. 'Maybe it's just the
dreadful uniforms,' she was thinking, 'or the late nights or
the food . . . Green bosoms? What on earth are they up to
now?'

'Tell you what,' she said suddenly, 'let's have some
chocolate. I had a food parcel this morning from Canada.
Turn up Canada again and I'll tell you all about it. And
Jessica, love, you take the box round. Five each and stop
squealing the lot of you. They're probably antediluvian.
They've been three months in the post.'

I really absolutely loathe girls who get keen on mistresses.
They make me ill. But I do very much like Miss Pemberton.
She has about the best sense of anyone I've ever met.

7

I will now proceed in letters. For a time.

Dear Jessica,

Sorry to hear you are ill. At least I suppose you are ill since you've been away for three days though when I called at your house yesterday Rowley just said, 'She's all wite' and swung his leg at me when I tried to come by. He said your father was whiting and your mother was at evensong and you were all white. I said do you mean all white or all right and he said ALL WITE and slammed the door. I should think he's getting it too. I'll leave this on the gate in a crack in a stick as usual.

Nothing's happened at school. It's still awful weather and we've got to stay in. I bet you got ill going to old Philemon's on Monday morning. She's mad. I saw her and old Crake standing on the promenade in all the rain today, just talking and talking. They were having to simply yell and their clothes were all behind them and their heads were going under their hats. I

heard old Dobbs say to Miss Pemberton, 'behold the
blasted heath', and they laughed though I don't know
that it looked much like a heath.

We have started knitting scarves for airmen while
she reads *The Cloister and the Hearth*. She says why not
choose an airman you know and it will get on quicker –
an uncle or a cousin. Do an inch and then pin a piece of
paper with his name on, so we all did and Cissie
Comberbach pinned on HENRY DROWN and Miss Dobbs
said That's enough Cissie YOU NEEDN'T TRY TO BE
FUNNY and Cissie cried because she really has got a
cousin called Henry Drown. They seem to have funny
names in that family. Miss Dobbs had to say she was
sorry. I have pinned Alexander Alabaster on my scarf
and I'm waiting till she sees because my father once did
know someone called that he was his best man.

Hope this amuses you on your bed of pain.

Lots of love from Florence Alabaster Bone.
P.S. Saw that queer woman again who was in Elsie
Meeney's talking to some soldiers. I think she's a spy.
P.P.S. Helen has got a BOYFRIEND !!!!!!! He's all spots.
He's much smaller than she is !!!!!!!!!!!!!!!!!!!!!!!!!! etc.

Dear Jessica,

Sorry to hear it's tonsillitis but you aren't alf lucky
because it's foul weather and we get soaked in train-line
and going up to dinner and I've got a filthy cold and so
has everyone else. Old Dobbs keeps blowing great long
tunes into her handkerchief. Blow bugle blow, set the

wild echoes flying, blow bugle, answer echoes dying,
dying, dying, and that's what I'm doing dying because
it's so COLD. That poem by the way is by Lord
Tennyson. I don't think he really was a Lord but his
mother called him Lord like I'm called Florence and
you're called Jessie-Carr and Cissie's cousin is called
Henry Drown. Then people would think he was a real
Lord (like Prince Littler, but I think he really is a prince).
When I have a son I'm going to call him Field Marshall
and then Monty will meet him one day and say 'Hallo
old man, weren't you with me in the desert?' Ho ho.

I hope this letter makes you smile which is probably
difficult with tonsils. Your mother told my mother in the
fish queue that it was a quinsy and I told them at school
and someone wet said 'Fancy having quins–es' Ho, ho
and once again ho. Miss Dobbs said Nothing to be done
with tonsils but keep warm and wait for them to go
down – and then HAVE THEM OUT! She says you will be
getting BEHIND and I have to send you books, and I said
with a beautiful innocent Wisage, shall I send her *The
Cloister and the Hearth*, and she turned very black and
began twitching and said, 'I think that would be
excellent.' But I've forgotten it so I'll bring it tomorrow.

Lots of love,

F. Field-Marshall Bone.

Dear Jessie-Carr,

Here's another letter. Aren't I kind. It's time you
wrote back. You don't get quinsies on your hands.

I was just coming back from getting your *Cloister and the Hearth* which I'd forgotten again and I banged into Miss Philemon taking her short cut through the shoe-bags. Now, LISTEN TO THIS. I've been in her flat. So you aren't the only one.

She said, 'Hello, you're in a rush my dear.' (Actually I'd knocked her down. She's awfully little have you noticed?) Her case had spilled all over the floor and I helped her gather it up. All the books didn't seem to fit in again and so she said I could help by carrying some home. Helen came too because she'd just come back from train line because she'd forgotten her sweet coupons.

Well on the way she asked why I'd still been in the shoe-bags and I said I'd forgotten a book for you and she said, 'Poor child! Is she ill? What book are you taking her?' Then she said, 'Is that a book she is particularly fond of?' and I said, 'Well no.' (Oh ha and ha!) and *she* said well let's find her an extra. So we went into her flat and I don't know *what* you were on about because it's lovely. I thought you liked things a bit messed up. She'd got a big fire on and everything and books everywhere. And what you meant about those green bxsxmx I don't know. It certainly is a funny sort of picture but it's not at all like you said and if you don't mind my saying so it's not disgusting unless you are feeling peculiar in some way. In fact I asked her about it (Helen just looked!) and she said, 'My dear, I expect you think it's hideous. I'm sure I would have done at your age. But do you know, it makes me feel so calm – to think that people do just live in the sun, picking fruit, dreaming about. It was painted in the South Seas you know. The sun shines on the people there all day long, from the minute they are born. 'Now take this to Jessica, and this and this,' and she picked out these books and I must say they do look pretty funny even if the bxzzzzzzxmz don't. I missed my train and I hope we don't get in a row like that fuss after Elsie Meeney's. It'll be Miss P's fault but she'll have forgotten by now that she ever asked us. You needn't return the books. She'll have clean forgotten. Or dirty forgotten. But she's NOT dirty and the picture's smashing.

Buckets of love from Florence Green-Bosoms Bone
P.S. Helen says it isn't her boyfriend. It's her cousin who's evacuated from Coventry. He looks as though he ought to be sent there. Ha!

Dear Field-Marshall Henry Bosoms Drown,

You are a clot. Tennyson was a real Lord. They made him one. And how dare you mention splendour falls on castle walls in the same breath as filthy Dobbs? And I hope her cold's as bad as my quins which are pretty well sextuplets or whatever they're called. Tonsils like footballs the doctor says but thank goodness going down now and they'll never get round to taking them out, not with air-raids and so on, so Dobbs can stop hoping.

The Maniac

Well I feel much better today, actually since after your last letter. It must have cheered me up. I'm very glad you liked her picture. I never said it *was* disgusting, I didn't get much chance to see it actually. I was in a bit of a state. I expect it was the quins coming on. Actually I'd rather like to see it again. It seemed a funny picture for her to have somehow, that's all.

Did you look at the books she sent? There's one about a man who decided to give up his whole life and paint pictures in the South Seas. He left his dull old wife and his children and everything. He'd got cold and bored and he went off and lived in the sun until he died in a mud hut painting natives. I should think it is the bosoms man. You would have to paint really marvellously for it to be all right. I wonder where his pictures all went? I wonder if you can see them, or any copies anywhere. Could you ask her if you see her?

The other books did you see? are *Romeo and Juliet* (!!) and some poems by a heavenly-looking man (there's a photo) called Rupert Brooke, but he only seems to write about fish.

See you soon. Back next week I spec. Yes R. has got it and serve him right, love, Jessica.

xxxxx from the quins.

Thursday P.S. Please will you give encl. note to Miss P. P.P.S. R. Brooke went to South Seas too. Fishing I suppose.

Tuesday December 10

Dear Miss Philemon,

Thank you very much indeed for sending the books with Florence Bone. It was very kind of you to think of it.

I have not yet read *Romeo and Juliet* but I have very much enjoyed *The Moon and Sixpence* and think that the hero sounds a very interesting man. I also have enjoyed the Poems and Memoir of Rupert Brooke and the extracts from his letters. He seems to be a very interesting poet and must have done a good deal of travelling. He seems to have been very good-looking.

I will return the books when I come back to school which ought to be quite soon now.

Thank you again,

Yours sincerely,

Jessica M. Vye.

Part II

The Boy

8

My father is quite old enough to be a vicar or even a bishop but having started late he has to begin at the bottom, and we live in an awful, narrow house in a terrace on the main road. It has a scrappy bit of garden in the front and a mean sort of yard at the back with high walls all round so that you can't see the neighbours' washing, only your own. There is hardly room even to hang the bedsheets in the yard and you have to bat your way through them, damp on either side, if you want to get at the coalhouse or into the air-raid shelter.

The vicar, who is an old, old bachelor, lives in a sort of mansion beside the church, keeping as much as he can to one room and wearing bedsocks and a great many rugs round his back to keep off the draughts. All over the top floor of the vicarage he arranges his apples, row upon row, in armies, and on the top landing he dries tobacco which hangs like bats on enormous frames. There's miles of cellars too, and a state dining-room cold as a station waiting-room where the parish council meets as seldom as it possibly can.

Our house has no dining-room at all because my father

has made it into his study. We eat in the kitchen. We haven't got a sitting-room either because mother's turned it into a sort of warehouse, full of things for the next bazaar, costumes for the Church Players, surplices with tears in that one day she will mend, bundles of old parish magazines, an old lectern, a set of dreadful candlesticks, the size of men, with electric bulbs in them instead of flames and an immense altar frontal of velvet and gold braid, big enough to carpet the passage and it would make the whole house a good deal warmer if it did. If you say to mother, what's wrong with the vicarage for all this stuff she says, 'I like to have things where I can see them, then I don't always have to be flying out.' This is a very odd remark because there is no woman anywhere in the world who flies out like my mother.

When you open the half-glass inner front door of our house – in the vestibule (the VESTIBULE. Nice.) there is generally a smell of burning and you run like mad into the kitchen at the back and fly with a saucepan into the back yard, or turn off the oven and fling open all the windows. Then you look round for the note which is in a different place every time but always says the same sort of thing, viz: 'Just remembered S.P.G. meeting – prayers for Fallen France, Love Mother' or 'Just seen clock Mothers' Union Celebration (not a party. Holy Communion). Please turn down Reg. 2, 25 past, then No. 9 last ten minutes. Must do vestments St. Simon and Jude.'

My mother's very new to the job too and finds it much harder than father. She was marvellous at being a schoolmaster's wife, going to Founder's Day in a hat and helping with the Old Boys' dinner and drinking coffee with the other wives in nice, plain, good-taste sitting-rooms and giving little supper parties. I used to go down at those when they'd all left the table and were back laughing across the hall and have the pickings. There were gorgeous little pork pies with cress round them in silver dishes borrowed from the School. We had a maid then, not much of one – not all that clean. She used to loll about the kitchen at night painting her finger nails, but mother had a lot of free time, and had her hair done. She wasn't bad looking then.

She's got a bit red in the face now and rather wild, slamming and crashing about and her clothes are vile. It does no good telling her and to tell you the truth I try not to think about what she looks like with her hair all frizzed all over her head and her red hands. When she gets angry she seems to grow knobs all over her face. I just never tell her about things at school like Speech Day as a matter of fact, I just say she's much too busy to come. She never asks. There just might never be a Speech Day for all she cares. When I'm at school I might just as well be dead for all the interest she takes, and I hope she finds this book and reads what I've said.

Father doesn't come to Speech Day either, but hardly anybody's father does. I'm quite glad actually that he doesn't think of it because he does stand out and sings so loud in the hymns. He would boom back the bits in the prayers where you answer the Headmistress and even if he didn't wear his dog collar which he often doesn't there's no mistaking he's a parson. It's funny really how quickly he's caught it. And he does talk!

He's a huge man, my father, with very thick grey hair and BURNING eyes and his face has very deep lines all over it. A lot of the day he sits in this terribly dark study that used to be the dining-room with his face in his hands pushing his fingers up and up through his hair until he looks like Moses on the mountain top. Then all of a sudden, he pulls his typewriter forward and starts clattering away like a concerto – sermons or articles for the newspapers (he's pretty famous). His sermons as a matter of fact are absolutely marvellous and the church is always much fuller for him than for the vicar. The congregation think my mother's a bit of a joke – they watch her flying about and tying herself in knots and you can overhear them saying things like 'I don't think she's had them bedrooms out in a twelvemonth' and 'You should see her back kitchen,' but my father they come and hear in absolute droves.

The thing about my father is that he can prove every single thing he says. He looks everything up and writes down where it comes from. He'll look up the meaning of a word right back to the beginning – to cave men almost. 'Hey, Jess, listen to this,' he says, then starts in on Old-Icelandic, Primitive Germanic, all sorts. I should think he probably knows more than Miss Philemon. 'Always check your facts,' he says, 'and check them now, not tomorrow-afternoon-if-you-happen-to-have-the-time.'

He says a great deal most of the time, and he sings a lot.

'The Lord of HOSTS is with us,' he'll sing to the cat on the stairs, 'The God of JACOB is our refuge.' He'll walk down the High Street and see the poor old butcher standing on his step with a great empty slab and he'll sing 'Forty days and forty nights' very sorrowfully. 'Never mind, Mr Slatford. It's worse in Russia.' He spins the old ladies round coming out of Matins and thunders out the Wedding March and sends them off all pink in the face. He wears any old clothes – a cloak sometimes! – and when he's on duty at the wardens' post he drinks masses of beer. Quite a lot of people don't think he's at all the thing but quite a lot of people absolutely adore him. Quite a lot as a matter of fact seem to be actually in love with him.

'I wish he'd come up and talk to me,' I thought one afternoon when the quinsy had been on the go for about a week. I was alone in the house, warm enough and not feeling too bad really with two hot water-bottles and a bottle of Lucozade and temperature nearly down. I had finished Miss P's books except for *Romeo and Juliet* which I couldn't get into. I had read *The Moon and Sixpence* twice and Rupert Brooke thousands of times. (I had got the Rupert Brooke propped open at the photograph on the table, keeping the page back with the Lucozade.)

I was down to my brother Rowley's comics and *The Girl's Own Paper* and I was bored. Mother had said, 'You could sew this alb for me. I don't know what the vicar *does* with his albs!' I said, 'What on earth's an alb? I can't sew anyway, you know I can't.' 'You could try,' she said. 'You are a silly girl. You could make such pretty things for yourself if you could sew, instead of having to have that awful stuff of Katie Binge-Benson's and Auntie Nellie's.'

'Why don't you then?' I said. 'Other mothers make things for their children. You only sew up old albs and stuff.'

'I can't make things any more than you can. You know I can't. I was a silly girl too. Anyway I hate home-made clothes.'

'You're just contradicting yourself.'

'Now that will do.'

'Well you are. Why don't you ever *think*?' I turned over to the wall. 'You just open your mouth and let your tongue wag about.'

'How dare you, Jess! If I'd talked to my mother like that . . .'

I called, 'Are you going to the Library?' but her feet were making a great noise on the stairs and she didn't hear. The front door banged.

'And now we'll wait for the explosion,' I thought. 'I wonder what this time? Hope it's not hard-boiled eggs like the time they all went off like pistol shots and one got stuck on the spout of the kettle. Gosh, that was some smell. It lasted a week.' Then I thought how even so it would be lovely to have a hard-boiled egg. Or two. Think of having two! I could remember when there was nothing in it — having two hard-boiled eggs. The blankets were warm and I sank into a nice doze. 'I think I'll dream,' I said.

I had been dreaming lately about Rupert Brooke — I'd found I could look for hours and hours at the photograph and the way the very thick hair went in to the back of the neck; but now I thought I'd have a change. I moved into a wonderful country.

A great white house stood in green fields. It was a long way off but it was still huge. A road, a smooth white road, went up to it on the right and then turned at right-angles up to the great front door which had a semi-circle of glass above it and a curved semi-circle of steps below. I floated up these, through the door into a marble hall with its black and white squares on the floor and a great white curving staircase, and sunshine pouring through the long staircase window and from a round glass dome in the roof, so that your eyes dazzled. I drifted up the stairs and looked on to the garden that stretched away into the distance where you could see beyond the tall, blue trees and lavender hills. Roses hung pale and heavy and sweet in the garden and there were old green statues. It was a still, hot, sparkling summer morning. Now I was in the garden, looking up at the back of the house which was clean and old, with roses showering round its windows, bees droning in them. A marvellous white dog with silky hair tiptoed out on to the lawn and sank down upon the grass. Through the windows you could see sofas and chairs of pale yellow satin and . . .

Ping!

and . . .

Piiiiiing!

I heaved myself up and got out of bed and wrapped the shreddy old eiderdown round me and waddled across the room. Then I woke up. What was I doing? I was ill. I didn't need to answer the door. I waddled back and got into bed again.

Piiiiiiiiiiiiiiiiiiiiiiiiiing!

'I'm not going. It'll just be some old Mrs Thing. I'm not going.'

Off it went again for about two minutes.

'Well, I'd better.' Out I got, settled the eiderdown, found my slippers and set off. I caught sight of myself as I got to the mirror and thought I didn't look too bad, so I tried out a more suffering sort of expression and straggled my hair. (One thing about the people here, they're all mad on illness. They give you masses of sympathy and send you soup and custards and stuff.) I picked up a scarf that was lying about and fastened it round my head tied at the top. I looked pretty terrible now and I set out for the stairs.

As I reached the top stair a letter fell through the letter box flap on to the floor and a shadow through the glass door – Ma had left the outer door half open of course – disappeared and went clumping off. I rushed down and looked at the letter which was thick and important-looking and very clean. 'I'd better see who it was,' I thought and opened the door on to the icy weather and peered along the road. I was just in time to see someone, a man or a tall boy or someone, flick round the corner and there was something about the back of his head that was familiar. But he was gone.

I shut the door, scrapped the eiderdown and went into the kitchen. I looked in the oven and found a stew bubbling quietly. There was a pan of cabbage simmering on top and some potatoes getting near the end for water. I topped them up and opened a few windows. I poked the fire and warmed my feet on the bending metal fender and sat down on it, watching the flames in the tarnish. 'Mother's nuts,' I thought, 'having a fender you've got to polish. It's just one more thing.' It was quiet and nice in the kitchen – queer to be downstairs again.

I looked down at the letter in my hand. 'MISS JESSICA VYE', it said.

9

'Well I never! Miss Jessica Vye. Who on earth?'
I turned the letter in all directions. 'No stamp.
There's nobody with paper like this. It's thick as cardboard.
Whoever is it?'

I smelled it. It smelled of nothing, but very clean. 'The
writing's a bit mingy. Perhaps it's from the vicar. But why
should the vicar write to me? Asking me to do the beastly
hymn-boards again most like.' I opened the envelope and
pulled out a thick, shiny, white card.

Mrs Archibald Fanshawe-Smithe
requests the pleasure of the company
of
Miss Jessica Vye
at a Children's House Party
at The Rectory, High Thwaite,
from Friday, December 20th
until Saturday, December 21st

R.S.V.P.

Underneath it said

> Bus leaves Cleveland Sands bus-station 1.20 p.m.
> Friday, returns Thwaite Lane End Saturday, 2.30 p.m.
> Bring additional clothes for snow-balling, Saturday a.m.

'Snowballing,' I said out loud. 'How'd she know it's going to snow? It sounds like a children's book. Who is she anyway? She's very good at working things out if she knows it's going to snow. What's she mean, House Party?' I stood on the fender and put the card up on the high mantelpiece behind the three brass monkeys and a broken clock used for teaching Rowley to tell the time and a couple of diseased old palm crosses. I caught sight of myself in the mirror with the scarf tied on the top of my head and I examined myself. 'I am sunken-eyed,' I thought, and I drew down my mouth and rolled my lower lip outwards so that the shiny part showed and blew air into my cheeks at the same time. This is something I have a habit of doing when I am alone. 'Spare a copper for a pore ol' woman,' I said. 'Me gel's goin' away tilt Big 'ouse, a-snow-balling with the gentry.' Then I fell off the fender and the cat went streaking under the cupboard. 'Eeeeh, I's got' t'fever!' and I tottered out of the kitchen feeling for the walls. I can never do anything like this when we have to stand up and do *Midsummer Night's Dream* at the front of the class for old Dobbs.

'Actually,' I heard myself saying in my ordinary voice in the passage, 'I do feel a bit funny.' I gathered up the eiderdown, rolled upstairs and back to bed where I slept till dinner.

It was a week later – oh quite a week – and I was sitting in a clear patch in the so-called sitting-room writing to Florence Bone when there was a terrible shriek from the kitchen. I took my left hand out of my hair and thought, 'Now what?'

'For goodness sake!' came father's voice from the study. We both came into the passage and saw mother, her face brick red and covered with knobs, holding the piece of cardboard in her hands.

'When did this come? What on earth is it? Why didn't you tell me?'

'I don't know,' said father. 'Let's have a look-see.'

'Oh that,' I said, and started back to my letter.

'Mrs Archibald Fanshawe-Smithe – that's old Fan's wife up at Thwaite. Well I never, what's she up to? Poor old Fan!' He began to laugh like mad. 'House party, by Gad! Whatever next!'

'Well, I can see it's from Mrs Fanshawe-Smithe, but . . .'

Father rocked and roared. 'Well I never! My stars. God is working his purpose OUT as year succeedeth YEAR!'

'But I don't see . . .'

'Don't suppose you do. You didn't know the Fanshawe-Fiddles at Cambridge for which my lamb and my love may you be truly thankful,' and he went back into his room and shut the door. He began to sing Jesus bids us shine with a pure, clear light and after a bit there was another great bellow of laughter.

Mother came into the sitting-room with a very determined step. 'Now then,' (she sat down) 'you will please tell me when this invitation came, why I was not told about it, and why you hid it behind the clock.'

'I didn't. I like that!'

'It was absolutely out of sight in a whole lot of clutter. If I hadn't decided to give the kitchen a really good do . . .'

'I wish you hadn't.'

'What did you say?'

'Nothing much.'

'You said "I wish you hadn't", didn't you? I suppose that means you don't want to go.'

'I don't know. I haven't thought about it.'

'Oh yes it does. I know you, Jessica. We're going to start a tremendous to-do now for the next week, sulks and slams and grumbles just because someone's been kind enough . . .' Well you know the sort of thing so I won't go on.

'. . . meet some nice new people,' she ended up.

'I didn't say I didn't want to go.'

'And what excuse am I going to make? I can't say we'll be away. Parsons can't say they're going to be away at Christmas.'

'Perhaps she won't know.'

'Won't know what?'

'That parsons don't go away . . .'

'Well since she is one herself.'

'She's a parson! Crikey.'

'No, no, no. Do listen. Her husband's one is what I mean.' (This conversation is absolutely typical of my mother. You can hear this sort of thing in our house every day of the week.) '. . . If you'd only listen. Oh dear . . .'

'I don't know what a Children's House Party is anyway,' I said after a minute. We glared at each other.

'Neither do I.'

She began to laugh and as a matter of fact I joined in and father shouted 'For the Love of *God*!' through the wall, and then more politely, 'For the Love of Mike must you make such a row?'

'Let's think about this then, Jessica,' she said a bit quieter. 'Now I do think you ought to go, dear. They're quite different from the usual run round here and they live in a lovely house. He's the Rural Dean you know – much older than she is I believe, but, oh, much nicer. They've got dozens of children but they're all at boarding schools so you've not met them. They're quite a different kettle of fish from the High School. Now I want you to go, Jess.'

'What's wrong with the High School?'

'Oh nothing's wrong with it. It's just that, well, it's nice for you to meet a different *type*.'

(She does this. Just when we start to talk she says something really awful like this. It makes me absolutely wild.)

'What on earth,' I said, 'are you talking about? You must be mad. There are thousands of different types at the High School, and a lot better types than . . .'

'Yes but . . . Well dear, no. It's wrong to say it but there is a difference. Boarding-school children do have a sort of *something*.'

'What do they have?'

'Well it's hard to say. But I think you'll see. It's a sort of *poise*.'

'You ought to see Iris Ingledew. Or even Helen Bell come to that, when she's sitting down at a piano. She's got so much poise she's nearly falling over backwards.'

'No, Jessica. These people do have *something*.'

'Sounds like money. If they've got thousands of children all at boarding schools.'

'No, no, they haven't got money. You'll be surprised. They wear terrible clothes and hardly have anything to eat. You'd think they were nobody if you met them on a walk – until you look again and you see they have this – something. Oh, they must make real sacrifices to send their children away to good schools.'

'Well I'm glad you don't.'

'We couldn't. We haven't anything to sacrifice. And anyhow your father wouldn't hear of it – it's quite against his principles. He would have a fit if he knew about even the shilling dinners. It is different for us.' She got up and went quickly to the kitchen and immediately turned round and came back again. Her hair had frizzed up and she was all knobs again. 'As a matter of fact they *have* got money. You'll see, Jess – you'll see. They'll go talking on and on about having no money. Never discuss money, it says in all the books of rules but they never talk about any blessed thing else. 'Penniless', they'll say and 'pass the salt' and it'll be in a Georgian silver salt cellar. Just you see if I'm not right. Just you see when you go.'

She was crying or something pretty like it. 'Crikey,' I said, 'whatever's wrong?'

'Nothing.' She sniffed and vanished into the kitchen.

'Well you needn't worry,' I shouted through, 'I'm not going.'

'Yes you are,' she shouted back.

'No I'm not.'

'FOR THE LOVE OF HEAVEN!' came out of the study.

'Ma,' I said, standing at the kitchen door, 'I'm not going. They sound frightful people. You're a fool even to think of letting me.'

'If I'd called my mother a fool . . .'

'Yes, and I bet the Fanshawe-Fiddleshaws never call their mother a fool either. They're all sweetness and light and lies and slop. I can't bear people like that. I'm not going.'

'And I can't bear insolence and rude girls hardly thirteen.'

'Too bad. I'm not going to stay with people you hate.'

'I love you, I love you,' she said with a hop (she's mad). 'You are going to the Fanshawe-Fiddleshaws and that is that. Anyway, I want to hear all about them.'

Back at school the next Monday everything was different. I had been thinking how different I was, and that they would notice – I was doing my hair in a new way. I combed it down all round without a parting, even over my face and tied a ribbon, or anything really, round my scalp, and then wound the hair backwards all round into the ribbon, like a lampshade. Also I'd grown by being in bed, and my face it seemed to me had an old look about it. I felt like a very old sister of myself, of the J. Vye who'd been to see the Head for instance. I felt – something or other. I don't know. Just older.

But nobody noticed. It was nearly half way through the first day that somebody said, 'Oh Jessica's back?' Even Florence looked unconcerned, sunk deep in thought and moody.

'They're all moody,' I thought. 'What's the matter with them? Quarrelling too. Must be the weather or something. And half of them talking about boys.'

I said, 'Florence, why's everyone different?'

'Mmm?'

'Everyone's different.'

'Different?' (It was really ding-dong conversation.)

'Were you talking, Jessica?' (Miss Pemberton) 'Oh, Jessica! You're back. Goodness me! Are you better?'

'Yes thank you, Miss Pemberton.'

'What were you talking about just then?'

'Oh I was just, um . . .'

'Well don't just um. Tell me what you were saying.'

Before I'd have said I couldn't remember. Now I said I thought everyone was different. 'And *worse*,' I said.

'You need a tonic,' she said. Dottie in the desk in front of me spun round and grabbed a rubber and snarled, 'What are you talking about?' and spun back again.

'I know what you mean,' said Miss P. 'It's always the same this term in this form. You'll be better when you're in the seniors next year and when the spring comes.'

'I'd feel better if the heating was on,' said Florence. Miss P. got us all up then doing exercises beside our desks and a pretty sight we must have been, all in our top coats, and Cissie even in a pixie hood!

'What's been happening then?' I asked as we tramped up Ginger Street on the way to dinner.

'Oh nothing. We've finished *The Cloister and the Hearth*.'

'That's something.'

'And we've started *Cranford*.'

'What's that like?'

'Awful. We've only read two chapters but it's all about people dying in terrible pain.'

'Well I suppose that might be more exciting than the other one.'

'No it's not. It's not exciting in the very least.'

'What about Helen's boyfriend?'

'He plays a queer instrument – a great big thing. He brings it to the station in a bag and walks home with her.'

'Whatever is it?'

'A cello or something.'

'Only women play cellos – all bow-legged and dreary. Queer sort of boyfriend.' Last term we'd have laughed and started pushing each other over but now we just trudged along in the snow. Cissie gave a great sigh – she seemed to be even smaller and wormier and looked even more tired. 'We never have snow in London until after Christmas,' she said, 'and then it's noice. We throw it araand and lark about. Not loik this dump.'

'Go back then,' I said. 'Why d'you come?'

'I had to. Me mother said.'

Joan said her mother sounded barmy. Florence said, 'Not barmy, bright. She was wanting rid of her.' But it didn't raise a smile and poor old Cissie just tramped along.

I said I'd been invited to this do in the holidays at High Thwaite and Dottie said, 'Oh lardie-da!'

'It's called a House Party,' I said. 'It's snowballing and stuff. Somebody madly organized who arranges for snow.'

'What's a house party?'

'I don't know. Opposite to a garden party I expect.'

'You can't snowball in the *house*.'

'I don't know what it's all about. It's some old vicar or something. What else has happened?'

'There's going to be a poetry competition. Miss Philemon came into English last week and took over and told us about it. First prize twenty pounds.'

'Help! Does it have to be long?'

'Nothing special. Not *Paradise Lost* or anything. Sort of school magazine stuff on anything to do with the war. It's a newspaper doing it.'

'A newspaper?'

'Yes, it's a competition for a children's poem – that's anyone still at school – eighteen or so. It's being judged by poets. I think they're pretty old ones who haven't been called up or anything, but real ones – Walter de la Mare I shouldn't wonder. It's *The Times* doing it.'

'The *Radio Times*?'

'Oh Jessica! *The Times*. Haven't you ever even heard of *The Times*? And your father a parson. Crippen!'

'We take the *Daily Herald*. What's *The Times*?'

'Well, it's very good. It's thicker than the others and they're all terribly brainy, the things in it. It costs 3d.'

'What – a day? No wonder they can give twenty pound prizes.'

'Miss Philemon wants everyone to go in for it and she'll pick out the best to send from the school.'

'Well, I'm not going in for it.'

'Why not?'

'I don't know.'

The next day at the end of English Miss Dobbs gathered up her books and said, 'Any poems yet?' and there was silence. 'Surely there are one or two. I'd like one from everybody really since Miss LeBouche says there will be no school magazine any more because of the paper shortage. The whole school is going in for it you know, Juniors and Seniors, and Miss LeBouche and Miss Philemon and I will be picking out the best. All the ones we send up will win a Book Token, and the one *we* think best will win a bigger Book Token, and we will pin it on the board in Big School. I should think this will be the last competition in the newspapers for years and years. Surely someone has got something ready.'

One or two girls began to bring bits of paper out of their desks and come up with them.

'That's right, Tessa. Oh good. Dorothy Hobson, that's a good girl. Thank you, Pat. Oh, hullo, here's Jessica back. I hope you will go in for the competition, Jessica.' You should have heard the effort she made to say that. She must have been listening to about half a million sermons to get that out.

I fixed her for a very long time (I've got these square eyes, pretty huge). 'I wouldn't write a poem now,' I thought, 'not now would I write a poem now that she's asked me, not if the Germans were saying they'd kill me. Not if they were saying they'd tear out my arms and legs from separate vans driving the opposite ways like the Polish refugees told Helen Bell.'

But it's funny how you can change your mind.

At the end of the afternoon we gathered up in the yard as usual for train line with a Staff to take us to the station and as usual set off up the road to the subway; but at the main road at the top of Ginger Street, near Elsie Meeney's café where there is a little parade of shops, a convoy of army trucks was going by very slowly. There were tanks and lorries, too, and queer things with machine guns and soldiers on top all covered in nets and branches, then great trailers with bigger guns and at the end a long, long column of marching men tramping four abreast and singing 'Roll me over in the clover' which set Dottie sniggering fit to die.

'We'll have to wait for this,' Miss Macmillan called out. 'I hope we don't miss the train. All right, girls, it won't be a minute.'

We were beside a dowdy little shop, in the front of the queue where I was — an art shop, very desolate and dusty. The windows were all criss-crossed with sticky paper in case of gun-blast from the cliffs. The main window was even more thoroughly done than the rest, with black sticky macintosh stuff all over it except for a square cut out in the middle. I leaned myself against the window and looked vaguely in through the square.

There was a picture inside of some sand on the edge of a bright sea and some men moving over it on horses. They were brown men, wet and thin, trotting in a clump. There were some bright, bird, god-people on grey horses on the left. One angel bird, god-man, I don't know what, was dressed in yellow. And the sand was rhubarb-coloured like the sunset. I set off into the shop.

'Here we are now,' cried Miss Macmillan, 'everybody cross. Gently now – you still have three minutes. Don't RUN. Don't PUSH for goodness sake. Jessica, what on earth are you doing?'

'I'm just going in here.' I was in trouble with the doorhandle. The train-line streamed past me.

'Into the art shop? Now? Don't be silly, you know you aren't allowed to go into shops in the town, and certainly not in train-line.'

'But it's Friday.'

'I don't see what that has to do with it. The weekend hasn't begun. Off you go,' and she shovelled me over the road.

I stopped in the subway and turned round, really wild and stamping (you can with her). 'Why can't I go? I don't see why I can't go.'

'Because you can't. Shoo! And for goodness sake Jessica don't make such an exhibition of yourself in front of the Upper Thirds. I'm surprised at you. You're behaving like a three-year-old.'

Old Dobbs would have frog-marched me to the station, and watched me on to the train, but Miss M. just turned away and set off home. Before I turned and ran for the train I saw her stop and look in the art shop window when she came to it, and because of this gift I have I knew what she was thinking. 'Nothing special here. A dusty old picture. Rather awful really. Some boxes of crayons. She could buy crayons at home. The place looks quite shut up. Funny girl. Queer picture. I wonder why the sand's pink?' Then she went off towards her tea without looking to see if I'd obeyed her.

I do really very much like Miss Macmillan.

10

'And anyway, thank goodness I didn't go in,' I thought at tea, 'because I hadn't got any money come to think of it. Not any.'

'Jessica's id a bood,' said Rowley.

'Not any money at all,' I thought.

We were all four together for once, father behind a book, mother making lists on the backs of envelopes, me staring ahead still wearing my school hat and my satchel and gas-mask at my feet where I'd dropped them off when I got in.

'Id a bood, id a bood. Jessica's id a holliboo bood.'

'You've got adenoids.'

'I haven't. So! What's adedoids?'

'Oh shut up.'

'Boody, boody, I hate you,' sang Rowley.

'You ought to be able to say horrible instead of holliboo by now. You're nearly five.'

'Boody, boody, I hate Jess.' He threw bread at me.

'Oh stop it!' said mother. 'Can't we be at peace for five minutes? Pick that bread up.'

Rowley got down and crumbled the bread into bits and

threw it in my face. Father lowered his book and began to roar and thump his fist.

'There are children in Germany starving for want of a slice of bread,' said mother.

'Serve them right!'

'Jessica!!'

'Well they started it.'

'For goodness sake, Jessica.' My father was very cold and stern. 'Just watch what you say. You are not six years old.'

'Always going on about age,' I said. 'Everyone's always saying I'm young. Well I am young. And I don't care.'

'Well Rowley's younger.'

'I never said he wasn't.'

'You taunted him. I heard you, Jessica. You taunted him about the way he speaks. A little child hardly . . .'

'Oh hell's bells and buckets of blood,' I said – this is the way we go on in our house. People just don't know what it's like in parsons' houses. If you read books about it – blimey! –

'Hell's bells and buckets of blood,' I said. 'Let's all go into a convent and pray.'

Father put down his book and clasped his hands together on the tablecloth (embroidered Michaelmas daisies – another thing we could do without. Another thing she has to iron every flipping Tuesday). He leaned forward over his hands with an understanding smile. 'Now then . . .' he said kindly.

'Oh stop being such a parson,' I said. 'Stop being so . . . pleased when I am difficult so that you can be understanding. You're only thinking of you, not me.'

His great big face went quite dead and he sat back. 'I don't know what she's talking about,' he said to Ma. 'I'll leave her to you. Goodbye. It's my Evensong!'

'I wanna come! I wanna come!' wailed Rowley; but father scooped him up and carried him out of the room. 'You go and play dressing up in the vestments.' He hugged him very tight and made ogre-noises into his neck and Rowley squealed with joy and disappeared into the front room.

After a bit I asked mother what she was doing.

'Just the Christmas pudding lists,' she said. I stared straight ahead and wound my legs round the chair legs and tipped back against the wall. '"If I should die,"' I recited to myself, '"think only this of me".' Not one of his best, actually. One of his smoothest but not one of his best.

> '"In Grantchester, in Grantchester
> There's peace and holy quiet there."'

Actually I'm not sure that's such a good poem either. There's something about it makes me feel very slightly – sick.

'Are we giving a lot of puddings away?' I asked.

'What a hope. We'll have trouble making just one for ourselves.'

'"In Grantchester, In Grantchester . . ."'

'I'm just making a list of things you need – the fewest. The things you can't do without really. Think of it, before the war I used to make puddings with seven eggs in! Think of it! And brandy. Half a gill! And we ate them with real cream. It's a wonder we weren't all balloons.'

'What's in this year's? "My name is Ozymandias, king of kings: Look on my works, ye mighty, and despair". That's a better poem. Harder, too. Firm. Better poet. "The lone and level sands stretch far away . . ."'

'. . . mashed carrots and potatoes, only don't tell your father. I hope it'll work. What *is* the matter Jessica?'

I dug about among all the things it was. 'Oh well,' I said, 'I just want some money.'

'What for?' She sounded surprised – almost pleased, as if she could talk about this.

'Masses of things.'

'Well, there's your birthday money. There must be a pound nearly, isn't there?'

'I want more than that. There's a picture I've seen.'

'Oh poor Jessica! Poor Jessica. Oh don't I know! Well I could lend you some, but actually I was thinking of the party.'

'The party? Surely I don't have to *pay* to go to that foul party?'

'No, don't be silly. I was thinking though that you might like some stockings. Silk stockings.'

'Crikey!'

'Though I have heard of a pair – a small pair that might do. I was going to say maybe with your pumps . . .?'

'My what?'

'Your pumps. Your black dancing pumps. You'll be wearing your pumps and your viyella.'

'WHAT!! Mother, are you stark, staring, raving . . . My viyella! I can't wear that. The waist's under my arms somewhere. It was too small in the summer. D'you think I'm a baby?'

'Well, my love, whatever else is there?'

I was stunned. I just sat. The picture I utterly forgot. I had never – you won't believe it – thought at all about what I was going to wear at this party. As a matter of fact I don't think I had ever thought about clothes in my whole life, unless of course it was plays. I don't think Florence ever thinks about them either – or Helen. Dottie does and all that lot. Joan doesn't. Cissie doesn't. You don't want to believe all you read in books about young girls.

Mother said comfortably, 'They'll all be in viyella. Don't worry. And the little ones will be in the big ones' cut down. It's the only good thing about the war – nobody can have better clothes than anybody else. You ought to be thankful.'

'I *bet* they won't be in viyella.' I can't tell you what a surprise it was to find how absolutely furious I was about this.

Rowley bounced out of the front room as I went by. 'Look at me,' he beamed, all loving, 'I'm grand as a king!' He was wearing a paper crown put out for one of the three kings next week and a trailing red thing.

'Help!' said mother along the passage, 'I must wash those. I wonder if I ought to do it before the pudding?'

Upstairs in my room I fixed the blackout over the window and sat down and tried to write a poem. It got terribly cold and I kept getting up, first for an extra pair of socks, then for the eiderdown, finally for a pixie-hood because my ears and neck were freezing. My breath blew in clouds round the reading lamp. 'DESPAIR' I wrote on a clean piece of paper. Then I put a wiggly line underneath it.

'Can I have the gas on?' I called down through the floor.

'There's a coal fire down here,' she called back.

I decorated the wiggly line and turned it into leaves and berries. Then I put a face into the D and P and R and wrote underneath.

'My heart is like a ship in a great storm.'

After about five minutes more I put my head down on the paper. 'Viyella!' I thought, 'Lord, I can't go in viyella.' I sat up and wrote.

'How fast the ocean rush sweeps on my soul
How fast the current pulling from the shore
How dark and deep the pain within my breast . . .'

'And *pumps*!' I thought, 'Pumps! Only Ma would ever call them pumps. I bet she'll make me take them in that vile shoe-box of old Miss Thing's that came out of Jane Austen or something.'

'As ship-wrecked mariner calls on his god,' I wrote (or something of the sort).

'As merman weeping in a seaweed grove,
As sorrowing dolphin on a silver strand . . .
I stretch my hands and cry for life and love.'

I read this through and was extremely pleased with it. I wrote a few more verses and then went and looked in the wardrobe. The viyella hung like a dead bird. It had little round pale-blue flowers all over it and pearl buttons and puff sleeves. I went back to the poem and read it again. It was dreadful.

I tore it up and began again. This time it went better and when I came back to it after supper it didn't look too bad. I made some changes and looked at the viyella again.

Father called up through the floor – I'm over the kitchen. You can hear everything. 'It's Itma. Coming down, Jess?' I'll say one thing about my father, he forgets in about ten seconds if you've been rowing with him. I heard him turning the wireless on.

I shouted, 'Not yet.'

'Oh leave that homework,' he called. 'You've got the whole weekend.'

> '. . . wrecked mariner calls up his god
> My heart is like a vessel, water-chopped
> Cold in the chapping, clipping . . .'

It was useless. And all the poems I'd done in the holidays, so easily too. The thing was I just hadn't the faintest wish to write a poem at all. I hadn't got anything to write about. I was full of lead. It wasn't as if I was trying to win the competition or anything. I just really wanted to win a book token – not even the 'Bigger Book Token'. Then I could sell it or something and get the picture. And a dress.

I got some scissors and cut out all the lines one by one and began juggling them about to see if there were a way in which they would fit better. 'See old R. Brooke doing this,' I thought. 'See W. Shakespeare. I'm more like a jigsaw maker.

Or a safebreaker trying combinations.' 'Combinations,' I thought, 'I wish I could go to the party in combinations. I wish it was fancy dress. Oh!'

I put down the pencil and scissors and stepped out of the eiderdown and went straight downstairs and into the front room again, carefully closing the door against the wireless. When I came out I felt utterly joyful. I put my head round the kitchen door and said Goodnight and blew kisses. Father raised his hand for silence because the news had started. Mother looked up and I said, 'I say can I wash those things for you – or can I do the pudding while you wash them?'

'Goodness, of course. Do you think you can?'

'Well, I'm no good at washing. I'll have to try at the pudding.'

'But love, you don't have to . . .'

'Quiet!' father shouted, chin on chest.

'Well, goodnight then.'

When I got into bed I heard them saying how odd I was – my age, etc., never the same mood two minutes together and all that jazz. 'How long does this awful teenage business go on?' my father said. 'I'm sure I was never like it,' said Ma. 'I was a happy little thing. But they're different now. It's the war.' Father said, 'At least they aren't afraid of us. We really *know* our children now. They don't have secrets from us. I suppose that's good.'

'My parents didn't want to know me,' said Ma. 'They weren't the least bit interested in me.'

'I wasn't the least bit interested in my parents,' said father. 'I didn't want to know them.'

'I expect you did really. They were so nice.'

'I wasn't,' said father, 'I was a swine.'

They droned on. They amaze me all the time. They are like children.

11

One-thirty at the bus station meant one-forty outside our front door at the other side of the road, and sure enough along it came and in I got. I dumped my suitcase under the stairs and wiped the window and waved to mother and Rowley who were in the front-room window, mother with a sort of uncertain look. I bought a half return to High Thwaite, settled down in the rattly seat and cleaned a bigger hole in the mist on the window. I undid a toffee Rowley had given me as a farewell gift.

'Have I got everything?' I asked the trees as the bus turned inland. 'Gas mask, identity card, emergency ration card. Though mother said nobody ever took an emergency ration card when you went to stay, you always had to offer it – like always having to offer to pay for your seat when you went with somebody else's parents to the pictures. Hot water bottle in case they haven't enough, toothbrush, hairbrush, flannel, soap, tomorrow's pants, extra socks, extra cardigan, wellingtons for the snowballing, pot of jam for Mrs Thing and – hum – stuff for the party.' I suddenly wanted to read my book very concentratedly. 'Oh tomorrow. Tomorrow,

tomorrow. When the bus is going the other way. Oh will it come? Oh if it were tomorrow and I were back!'

I read my book but my thoughts wandered about for the next half hour. The bus got packed with workmen and was absolutely quiet except for heavy breathing and the clank of a tea-can as they eased their cigarettes out of their pockets, and great coughs now and then. The one next to me had the *Daily Mirror* open on his knee. There was a headline about the Blitz.

'London's in a bonny mess then,' he said, not looking at anyone.

'We's in a bonny mess anyways,' said another across the gangway, staring straight ahead. Their faces were sharp-looking, with hard skins and a lot of them looked old to be still working.

Near the steelworks all the workmen got out leaving a gritty smell behind them and a bit further on two or three country-looking women got in who had been up to Shields East to look at the shops. They were silent too. The bus conductress flounced along for their tickets and banged on the back of the driver's window to say move on. He turned and winked at her. She had black hair turned underneath at the back and rolled up in a backward sausage in front, and the front part was dyed yellow.

'Brazen,' a very fat woman said across the bus from me, surrounded by parcels. 'There'll be a rare shock for some when this war's over,' she said to the bus in general.

'If y're meaning me,' said the conductress, 'I've got two lads int' air-force so you can stuff it.'

'It's a bit of 'Itler as some folks wants,' said the woman.

'And we'll 'ave it lively, from't papers.'

'It's bein' so cheerful as keeps 'er goin',' the conductress said to me in particular and went singing up the stairs.

I was just wondering why the fat woman thought that Hitler would mind the conductress dyeing her hair when I saw we were stopping at the end of a lane with larch trees trailing their arms each side of it. There were some people dotted about (Oh God! Oh help!), some of them sitting on a sort of park fence and wearing bright red caps with pompoms on top. There was a collie dog, white and orange, and a dumpy little woman with her arms full of holly.

''Igh Thwaite End,' the conductress cried down the stairs. 'That's you, love. Can you mek out?'

'Yes, thanks.'

I got my case and stepped out and looked quite a long way back because we'd overshot. Under the black larches, on the bare road their arms and legs were thin like insects'. I put my case down for a moment. Then I picked it up and held the handle very firmly and stepped towards them, awkwardly because the case was big and grazing the frosty edge of the road. I thought, 'They're all arranged.' They were grouped all bright and lively under the larches. 'They look as if they're in a book.'

One of the children jumped off the fence with a happy laugh, sort of in tune, and called to the dog who began to jump and dance round her, higher and higher, springing beautifully into the air. 'That fat little woman'll be the cook,' I thought. Someone shouted 'Hurray', and I felt something touch my face and the same moment the little woman called out in an amused, pretty voice, like the laugh. 'There you are you see. It's snowing!'

'And there she is!' she added. 'Go along, you great boys. Go and get her case, poor angel. It's nearly as big as she is. Now – let me look at you. Jessica Vye! How *like* your dear father!' And she took me by the shoulders and stood back from me, holding me off, smiling with sort of triumph. She was plump, rather than fat. Pursy. She was *pursy*, with a pretty little mouth and a small neat nose, bright brown eyes and brownish-greyish hair drawn into a bun – no hat – and the snow was beginning to settle on it here and there in light large flakes. Her tweed coat had had nearly all the colour washed out of it years ago and thick goloshes on the end of stout little woollen legs. Her cheeks were pink, like cheeks reflecting a bright fire, and firm and shining with cold.

I thought, 'She does look exactly *like* a cook, but . . .'

'I'm not the cook. I know I look like one. I'm the hostess. And my dear, dear Jessica, I just can't stop looking at you.'

'Oh come *on*, mother,' said the girl who had laughed – a bit older than me. (Rosy lips closed over slightly sticking out teeth and RICH long brown hair.) She turned away and set off up the road. A stately tall boy said, 'Let me have your case.' He had glasses and a white freckly face like porridge.

'And *we* shall walk together,' said Mrs Fanshawe-Smithe, and linked her arm through mine. The other children took no notice of me at all and went running here and there ahead of us up the road calling to each other and the marvellous dog. Between the trees in the distance at the top of the lane the brown church tower rose up to meet us.

If there is one thing in the world I hate more than anything else it is having someone's arm linked in mine.

'We didn't bring the car down – not really worth it,' she said. 'We took it yesterday to meet some of the Harrogate guests – school friends of the children you know. They're staying longer. We have to be so careful of the petrol. It's just a nice walk so long as we have Giles for the suitcase. Now – tell me? How *is* your father?'

'Oh – he's very well, thank you.'

'He was such a live WIRE at Cambridge you know, long ago. And such a speaker. I expect he's a marvellous preacher, isn't he?'

'Yes, actually he is.'

'Of course. Quite wasted as a schoolmaster. My husband and I were delighted – quite delighted when he joined us.'

'Joined . . .?'

'Entered the Church. I expect your mother was, too. I've not met your mother.'

'I don't know really. I don't think she's got any time to really think about it.'

'Oh don't I sympathize! Don't I just sympathize! It is the hardest life in the world, child.' She dropped her voice as if she were telling a secret. 'The hardest life in the world, marrying into the Ministry. Now then, let's go and have a nice comfortable time before tea.' She dropped my arm (thank heaven). She bounced so much when she walked that it had been crazy. To walk just ordinarily had meant being jolted at every step, but bouncing alongside had seemed ridiculous. I had done the best I could trying to keep some sort of time, watching the goloshes and putting in a little slip step now and then when they went faster. I'd heard two of the little girls behind sniggering, but when I was free to look round they had faces like stones.

'And here we are!'

There was a huge metal field-gate, about eight feet long which swung slowly back on to a wide gravel drive. At the end stood an enormous white house with rows and rows of shining windows and a door with a shell over it made of glass. A great black cedar stood beside it with blots of black at the ends of its queer boughs, like lino-cuts. An immense see-saw stood on the lawn and from high up in the cedar hung the longest swing I'd ever seen. In the background was a big stone barn, and a paddock with large, park-like trees standing about it, and a pony underneath one of them.

'Yes – isn't it?' she said. I hadn't spoken. 'The church isn't much – Oxford Movement, 1840s. Horrible really. We took it for the Rectory. Of course – come in dear. Giles, take the case up. That's right, we'll warm in the library – of course when the Rector and I first saw it (we've hardly been here a year, you know) – we said 'Impossible! Out of the question.' We stood in the garden and said, 'Look at all those windows. Where would we get the blackout?' But do you know?' She riveted me. I just stood waiting. 'DO YOU KNOW? When we got upstairs – *shutters!* Beautiful eighteenth-century shutters, all the way along. There now? Warmer? Good. Off you go then with Magdalene and she'll show you where you're going to sleep.

'Tea in the kitchen,' she called musically again, from the foot of the stairs. 'Dining-room *firmly* locked until this evening. For we have much to do before the Great Occasion. And oh, Magdalene,' she added, 'when you come down, will you bring Jessica's emergency ration book, dear.'

Upstairs to wash, downstairs for buns and tea at a big scrubbed kitchen table, dozens of people running about and laughing and banging doors, upstairs again to get ready. I blinked and whirled. I even tried to shout and scream a bit with the rest. But what I wanted to do was to go away somewhere and be quiet. This queer woman who could thought-read like me. The odd way she talked to you as if you were her own age. These great big rosy girls, all so pleased with themselves. I went off into a lavatory for a bit, but it was no good. I knew I'd have to come out, and I was sharing a bedroom with the two younger girls who'd been behind me laughing in the lane – Sophie (if you please!) and Claire. Magdalene, who must have been about my age, had got a school friend already in her room. The two of them had gone off into it after tea and firmly shut the door. You could hear them laughing a good deal inside.

About me I suppose. I glowered across at Sophie who was watching me from a half-perch on the fireguard, legs not quite touching the floor.

'Is this your bedroom?'

'No. There's some friends of Magdalene's in our room. This is the day nursery. We've put up camp beds.'

'Day nursery? Aren't you a bit old to have a nursery?' (I was only trying to make conversation.)

They stared. 'It's just what it's called,' Claire said. 'It's the name of the room. It'll always be that. It always *was* a day nursery before we came. You can tell by the toy cupboards.'

I looked round. It was an enormous room with two great cupboards to the ceiling, big windows with wooden bars, looking out at the cedar tree, a fender with a brass top, a huge old rocking-horse, a huge old dolls' house, a shelf of beautifully-kept old dolls and another shelf of tidy books, mostly by Arthur Ransome. The paintwork in the room was so old that it was hardly there at all but scrubbed wonderfully clean. The brass door knob and finger-plate and the rail of the fireguard shone like silver in the firelight. Outside across the blackness of the cedar tree great white snowflakes were falling. In front of the fire was a big rag rug and there was a rocking chair with a floppy cushion on it and a ginger cat asleep on the cushion. Over the fireplace was a cuckoo clock. On the mantelpiece was a little chinaman with a nodding head, a poker-work matchbox holder and a drum of coloured spills. It was wonderful. It was warm. It was full of peace. I put my hands under my armpits because I wanted to hold my arms out to it. Don't ask me why I put on the filthiest face I could and said to Sophie, 'However do you manage to get the coal?'

'Oh we saved up for it for the party. We usually absolutely freeze. It's spiflicating now, isn't it? I suppose we'd better put the shutters up. It's getting dark. It's nearly black-out.'

'*Spif*licating?' I said.

'Yes, *spif*licating,' said Claire who'd been watching me all the time from the bed. 'Any objection?'

'Oh no,' I said. 'Sounds as if you've been reading Arthur Ransome or someone.

'Well we have. So what? Haven't you? He's whizz.'

'He's whizz,' said Claire, still watching.

'He's *spif*licating,' said Sophie. 'Don't you think?'

'I'm afraid I don't. I can't stand him.'

'Can't you?'

'All those pathetic adventures.'

'Didn't you even like him when you were our age – tennish and elevenish?'

'I'm afraid not.'

'Gosh!'

I went and stood looking out of the window. 'I'm vile,' I thought. 'I hate them. "*Day* nursery".' Coal fires in the bedroom. And that servant person at tea, and all those posh aunts and stuff. And that awful mother asking for my rations. Mother would never have asked, *never*. Heavens, when Auntie Nellie came and stayed a week we never took her ration card. And the way they talk – awfun for often, and atome for at home and Red Crawss, and all that laughing when they're not really amused. Because they're nobs. You can hear it isn't real. Shrieks of laughter and their eyes all cold. I wonder if the King and Queen are like that?

'Didn't you even read Mrs Molesworth?'

'No.'

'Or Mrs Nesbit?'

'I've never even heard of them I'm afraid. I don't really care for children's books.'

'Not even Beatrix Potter?'

I tried to curl my lip again but this time I couldn't and I muttered yes.

'Oh goodie, she likes Beatrix Potter,' Claire cried, clapping her hands and rolling about the bed. 'Lovely, lovely Nutkin. Lovely, lovely Patty-pan. Lovely, lovely Tailor of Gloucester, but oh so terribly *sad*!'

'What's your favourite?' asked Sophie weighing things up still across the room.

'Mr Tod.'

'Mr Tod – oh horrors! horrors!' squirmed Sophie.

'Why Mr Tod?'

'Because it's evil.' That shut them up. 'D'you mind if I go downstairs? I've left the book I'm reading at the moment in the hall.'

As I went along the landing I heard them at it – snorts and muffled shrieks of joy and 'Isn't she *gharsley*?' in Claire's voice under the pillow.

I found the book on the hall chest and my handbag which I'd forgotten I'd got with me. It was an old passed-down one of mother's from one of her rich friends – a grand sort of bag of real black leather with a shiny clasp. On the bus I'd felt pleased to be borrowing it, but now, seeing it on the hall table, I wasn't. It was for a woman, not for me. The rest of me was O.K. – jersey and skirt, knee length socks, school shoes. They were all in that sort of thing. 'And my hair's as good as theirs,' I thought. 'If anything better. And my face is as good as theirs – at any rate my teeth don't stick out like all theirs do and I don't have great iron bars all over them, even if they are big. My eyes are all right too.' I stood looking at myself in the lovely dim hall mirror. 'I look all right in this anyway. My eyes are like saucers – no, what was the third dog? Like towers. My eyes are like towers. I know I don't look all that awful. The station-master's always looking at me in train line, and there was the pris –' Instead of going on, though, I picked up the book and turned away with a sort of stomachache. 'Why can't I think about it? Why can't I? I could straight afterwards. It was nothing. Why can't I now? Think!'

But I only got as far as the leaves on the bank and some sun slanting into them.

There was a cough and a shadow passed along the end of the passage, against the shadowy window at the end. There was a glimpse – hardly a glimpse, just a sort of impression, of someone I knew walking away. But there was no one there. 'I'm going mad now,' I thought. 'I'd better go back upstairs. I suppose we'll have to get ready for this awful party.'

When I got back to the day nursery I found it empty except for the cat, so I took my sponge-bag out of my case and went off looking for somewhere to wash. Along the corridor was a huge freezing bathroom and after I'd locked myself in and fiddled with a queer ball arrangement in the basin, with a brass lever and taps above it, all marvellously polished, I took off my jersey and washed my top half and brushed my teeth and scrubbed my nails. Then I put my jersey back on and carried my vest back to the bedroom. I got out the viyella with a flourish and laid it on the bed. Then I got out a carrier bag and emptied the rest on to the bed and it slid and flowed about, all scarlet and gold. I looked down at it and then all round the room, and I asked the air which was right.

I didn't need to of course. The pale, washed-out viyella was absolutely right. You could tell girls had been putting on pale, pretty, nicely-made old party dresses in that room for about thirty thousand years. An *English* dress, as English as the patchwork quilt it was lying on, as English as the rag rug, as English as the books on the shelves. A dress whom England made, wrought, made aware, for girls at peace under an English heaven. If I should die think only this of me, I look as dreary as a cup of tea. And bla and bla and bla.

I looked at the other clothes – they were the black page's from the Nativity Play. I'd worn them last year when they were too big and had had my face blacked with cherry blossom. There was a gold tunic made from an old cope of the vicar's and a pair of scarlet tights. There was a gold turban, too, with a big purple brooch from Woolworth's but I hadn't brought that. The clothes shone from the bed in a violent heap. The room looked washed out. It turned pale at the sight of them. I put out my hand and touched the scratchy gold stuff and the jewels. 'You very . . .' There were the dahlias and the orange sunshine and the man's face all tears. 'Shut up,' I said and put on the clothes. 'I'm not afraid of these people,' I said. I tipped the cat off the rocking chair.

My red satin legs looked good on the fireguard. Oh *spifli-cating*. I settled down to *The Moon and Sixpence* third time through.

After ages there were voices outside of the girls coming back along the corridor, and the other voices of Magdalene and her friends and a great clattering and thundering on the stairs. 'But where is Jessica?' called the voice of Mrs Fanshawe-Smithe. 'Go and see, dears and I'll do her hair, too.' Sophie rushed in in her dressing-gown, her plaits undone and her hair loose down her back. 'Oh here she is,' she cried. 'Oh lawks!'

Claire came in. 'Oh,' she said.

Mrs Fanshawe-Smithe came in. 'Jessica, we lost you. I've been doing all the girls' hair in my bedroom. Shall I do yours? Oh! . . .'

'It's all right, thanks,' I said. I uncrossed my legs and got up. I felt marvellous.

'Jessica!' Mrs Fanshawe-Smithe put her hands up to her face and made her eyes enormous. 'Dear – how awful!'

I found I wasn't feeling too marvellous after all. I began to want to stand on one leg. I found I wasn't looking eye to eye at her any more, I was eye to foot.

'How awful! How awful of me. I let you think it was fancy dress! Oh you look so gorgeous too!'

Sophie and Claire left the room with a clatter and some snuffling and after a moment Magdalene came in. I saw her feet only (in pumps). 'I *say!*' she said in her fruity sort of voice, 'I say, you do look spiflicating!'

'I'll tell you what,' her mother said triumphantly. 'We'll all wear fancy dress. Do let's! What fun! I'm sure we can find something in the attics – the only trouble is there isn't really time . . .'

'Oh, but I want to wear my new viyella,' said one of Magdalene's friends who were crowding in the door. 'It took sixteen coupons.'

'So do I,' said another. 'Mine's a wool. I queued. And I queued for some tangee lipstick, too – in York all last Saturday morning.' 'I want to wear my silk stockings,' said someone else.

'Oh what *can* we do?' she appealed. 'I don't think I can bear it if Jessica takes off those glorious clothes.'

But you could see from her eyes she could and was thinking hard how to get it all straightened out quickly. She even looked at her watch.

'I am not afraid of these people,' I said to myself, 'I am not. I am not. I will not be like them just because it's easier for them. I don't care if they do laugh, I will look beautiful, I will, I will.'

'Magdalene, you are about Jessica's size, what about lending her your green? Oh what a good idea, she'd look lovely in green . . .

'Or my orange,' said Magdalene. 'She'd look better in orange and it's newer.' (She wasn't so bad, or at any rate she had stupendous manners.)

'Yes she would,' another girl said, 'and she can have some of my tangee.'

'Don't be ridiculous!' (charming laugh) 'Tangee indeed!

It'll be false eyelashes next. Not that she needs any of those – she has lovely eyelashes. And eyes. She has her father's marvellous eyes.'

Trying not to be sick on the mat I willed myself. 'I will wear these clothes, I will, I will. I will not let them win.'

'Actually,' I said, out loud. 'Actually I have got another dress with me. It's viyella. Just in case,' I said. 'Just in case it wasn't fancy dress.'

'Oh you are sensible! You really are. Dear me I shall be so sorry not to see you in cloth of gold ('My dear!' – next week to Lady Cheesecake, 'the daughter turned up in cloth of gold!') It does so suit you. There's the viyella – oh, yes, that's splendid. What a sweet, high waist. And your hair's all right? Yes – well. I'll go and change now shall I? Don't be long all of you. I'll just look in and hurry up the boys.'

12

High Thwaite Rectory,
North Riding of Yorkshire,
England, Home and Beauty.

Dear Florence,

Don't know why I'm writing to you as I'll probably
see you tomorrow or Monday, but I'm stuck at this
awful place and nothing to do, so it passes the time till
the bus goes this afternoon. For an awful moment when
I looked out of the window this morning I thought we
were snowed up, but it's only up here in the village.
The buses are still running and it's just a question of
walking to the lane end and I pray and I pray and I pray
that they'll let me. Thank heaven we're not on the
phone or I know she'd ring up (the mother) and ask if I
could stay on and if I have to stay here a minute longer
than they said at first I'll die.

It's the House Party I'm at – do you remember?
Snowballing. There *was* snow of course and everything
picture post-card. They're all terribly jolly. They all go

to some boarding school, the girls. Thank our stars we
don't. They're frightful. They call the new girls at the
school 'the new bugs' and they play CRICKET in great
big pads – I've seen them in the hall cupboard. They
have long hair they toss about and they clean out their
hairbrushes every Friday night at seven o'clock!!! They
write one letter home every Sunday afternoon from
3.30 to 4 o'clock, and the staff READ it before it's
posted. Think of that! You can't say if you're miserable
or how filthy old Dobbs is being. Just like writing an
essay. I'd go mad. I said so and they all looked at me
and said they'd hate to go to a day school, because
boarding school makes you Stand On Your Own Feet.

They're so conceited and they've done nothing. The
school's apparent(ant?)ly in the wilds and they've never
been in an air raid. There's no cinema and they've
never been in a public library. They never go out of the
school except to Church on Sundays like Jane Eyre or
something. They're like something out of the Girl's
Own P.

Funny thing, but at this party last night there were a
lot of aunts and friends of their mother's about called
things like Auntie Boo and Lady Pap-Fisher (honestly)
and they thought I was one of *them* and Auntie Boo
who was in Red Crawss (you have to call it Crawss)
uniform with a mouth like a safety pin and hardly ever
spoke suddenly said, 'Good thing these girls are away
from here, Barby. Raids getting no joke. Teesside,' and
Lady Pap-Musher said, 'But Boo-Boo (yes) you

couldn't send them to a local school *anyway*. I mean they're so *crowded* and nobody *does*.' I could see the mother looking at me and pretending to be embarrassed but really rather enjoying it (she's the ghastliest and she hates me) and so I suddenly said, 'How can they be so crowded if nobody does?' and there was the most terrible, horrible silence all round the room.

That was at the supper table – huge great dining-room. It was all very grand. Mrs Fanshawe, the mother, was in a *long dress*! The food was marvellous – they've got their own chickens and I suppose you can get butter and stuff in the country. We had turkey and trifle and ICE CREAM. I'd forgotten what ice cream tasted like – she made it herself. They've got a fridge. It was chocolate. I wish I could have got you some. I'd love Rowley to have some he's never tasted it. Well, anyway, after I'd made this great *gaff* about local schools there was suddenly a trembly, trembly voice from down the other end of the table, laughing very quietly all by itself. 'What was that Archie?' Mrs F-S called, and it was the father, who's the Rector, sitting down the other end just laughing away as if he was all alone or at the pictures or something. He's incredibly old with a long face very pale with freckles like national wheatmeal bread – there's a son, Giles, with the same face exactly, both very learned-looking with specs.

'Who is that child?' he said, the Rector. 'Hush!' said Mrs F-S, 'I believe Archie spoke,' and everyone was quiet. 'Who is that child – the child with the wild eyes,'

he said (me!) and she said, 'That is Jessica Vye, my
dear,' and *he* said, 'F. J. Vye's daughter. I might have
guessed,' and went on with this trembly, trembly laugh.

Well, (I hope you're enjoying this) then the dance
began. They've got a vast great room with a carpet
rolled up and the sofas pushed back and a piano in the
corner. Auntie Boo played it till it nearly burst – great
marches and things. We had a Paul Jones to get us
going but it was nearly all girls. Mrs F-S and the Nannie
sort of person and Lady Pap had to be boys, and one or
two of the big girls. The Rector disappeared and so the
only real boys were this speckly son and a couple of
nondescript friends and the verger's grandson who
arrived after supper and a soppy boy Lady Thing had
brought. Half the time I seemed to get opposite Mrs F-
S but we pretended I hadn't and grabbed just anyone.
She's one of those people who can read your thoughts.
We seem to be very uneasy in each other's company.

Well we did valetas and gay gordons and military
two-steps and hokey-cokeys and pally-glides and
Lambeth Walk. The verger's grandson suddenly
shouted out, 'Let's 'ave knees oop Mother Brown,' but
they pretended they hadn't heard.

Well all of a sudden I got awfully fed up with it all
and so I got near the door and slunk off. Actually it's a
lovely house. I wish I could be absolutely alone in it,
just walking and walking through all the rooms in the
moonlight. I walked down a corridor and up the back
stairs, and then I came down the main staircase again –

it's curving and it has lovely curly iron banisters with
roses and things. It would be marvellous for plays. And
then I strolled about until I got to the library where
we'd been when we first arrived and there was a coal
fire in there and the shutters back and the snow shining
in and over the fire in a chair with a high back there was
a boy. I nearly had a fit. I thought he was a ghost
because (don't tell *any one* this) he was absolutely,
exactly like Rupert Brooke. He was leaning forwards
looking into the fire with his chin in his hand and his
hands were very long and his wrists were very long,
too, sticking out of his jacket that was too small for him
and he had that marvellous face and his hair was
terribly long and thick – all round at the back like you
never see now, and you could tell it was the most
marvellous blond – you could even see in the dark,
what with the fire and the snow outside. He was better
than Leslie Howard and about 16 I think.

Well, I just stood inside the door and in the end he
said without even looking round, 'Who're you?' I said
Jessica Vye and he said nothing, just went on staring at
the fire, fiddling about, bashing at a log with a poker.
Then all of a sudden he said, 'Jessica VYE!' and got up –
he's terribly tall – and stood staring and staring at me. I
was in that foul ANTEDILUVIAN viyella I had last year,
with the waist nearly under my arms and the top of my
legs all fat, but he just stared and stared. I thought it
must be Romeo and Juliet or something (except that I
haven't read it) and I must say I just stared and stared

back. Then he said, 'Can I come and see him?' Just like
that! I thought, crikey! and I said yes, I supposed he
could and he said, 'When?' I said, 'Well any time I
suppose. Why d'you want to see my father?' and he
said, 'Because he is a Great Man.'

Just then there was a noise and a door opened and
people were calling things out and the piano started
God Save the King like mad. 'The party's over,' this
boy said. 'You'd better go back,' and he sat down again.
So I went away and we waved off the guests who
weren't staying the night, through the snow, and we all
went to bed. Magdalene – the sister – and her friend
talked for hours through the wall and giggled, and the
two I was sharing the day nursery with sniggered on a
bit, but I just shut my eyes and pretended to be asleep.
Actually he is the most heavenly, marvellous person
I've ever seen in my life and I didn't mean what I said at
the beginning of this letter that I'm having an awful
time, because I've never been so happy in my whole
life.

Love Jessica.

I finished and blotted the last page of this letter very carefully – it was in an exercise book that I'd got with me. I was
writing at one of those little desks with drawers all down
one side and a square of old green leather on top, which
faced the garden where I saw all at once that snowballing
was going on. I watched how everyone was running about,
dark sharp people on the soft snow against the rounded

bushes and the uphill lawns. Mrs F-S was there, very rosy, and even the Rector in a long sloppy coat over his cassock and two fawn mufflers. The little girls were leaping about the see-saw. Their breath was going up in blue puffs. The brown church tower went up behind them. It was happy and beautiful. I saw my mother, suddenly, in our cluttery kitchen, all in a flummox, pulling on a coat, over her apron, calling 'Freddie, look after Rowley for a minute. I've got to fly. I've forgotten . . .' And her awful hands. Sophie landed Giles a snowball on his glasses. 'Bravo,' cried the Rector clapping his hands leisurely in the air while Mrs Fanshawe laughed her tranquil laugh.

And I hated them.

I read the letter through from beginning to end and then I turned back to where it said that I left the party – 'Well I got suddenly fed up' or something of the sort (I've had to write it from memory but I have a good one) and I carefully tore off just above it: and then I tore everything that came after it into the smallest possible pieces. I found an envelope – one of the thick, clean ones the invitation had come in – which was in a little wooden rack thing on the desk, and I put all the pieces into it and put it up my knicker leg.

Then I took another envelope and addressed it to Florence Bone and put the half-letter in it just adding love from Jessica along the furry bottom edge, and as I stuck it up I felt somebody standing behind me in the door and I turned round. 'You coming for a walk?' he asked – the marvellous boy.

13

We unbolted a side door and crossed a snowy lawn and round behind the barn to avoid the front drive, but Mrs F-S spotted us climbing the hill. 'Christian,' she called. He turned and waved and then went steadily upwards with his back to them all and me following. We climbed an iron fence, skirted a few tombstones and then another fence and were out of the graveyard and climbing a sloping field up to a wood. 'Christian,' came his mother's voice more faintly. He paid no attention.

The wood had a path along its edge. The trees to the far side of it stood thick as the tubes of honeycomb. In among them, here and there, were black holly bushes. The snow on the path was like sugar and unmarked except by a few foot-marks of birds and it seemed to run gently on and on for miles along the ridge. At the other, open side of the path the country spread itself in a great plain as far as you could see, the slight hump of every field clearly marked by black hedges. By the shadows of the snow you could just see the difference between grass and furrow. The main road run-ning through this plain looked important and bigger than it really was because the traffic had churned it up into a brown slush stretching far away. Square blocks of trees stood here and there. The air was very clean and clear, even far away towards the steelworks and the sea. The only signs of people were the few great houses, each with its park, some with cottages round them. It was a hard, sharp, rough great place. I said 'Oh!' when I saw it.

'What d'you say?' asked Christian Fanshawe. He stopped and put his hands which were without gloves under his jersey. Then he shook them crossly. 'Whatsthematter?'

'I said 'Oh'. It's lovely isn't it?'

'What?'

'Well – this. All this.'

'Lovely? It's hell.'

'*Hell!*'

'Yes, hell. Ghastly place. It nearly finished off William the Conqueror, this place. Even a chap like him. He was lost on this place for twenty-four hours in a sea-fret, poor bloke. They still talk about people swearing like Billy Norman round here.'

'But why does that make it hell?'

He flung his yellow hair about and went stamping off ahead again. 'Because it's waste, isn't it?'

I thought about it. 'Well why not, what's wrong with waste?'

'Look,' he said stopping again. 'Have you *seen* the places round here? Have you ever seen the slums? Have you ever been round the streets in a place like say Cargo Fleet – or Shields East or Sunderland or Middlesbrough?'

'No.'

'Well go. Take a look at them, go in a train and just look at them. You can see a good bit from the train. No lavatories, no bathrooms, no gardens. Back to back. Kids without shoes . . .'

'Oh go on,' I said, 'that's not true anyway. They do have shoes.' I remembered a sermon of father's talking about the days when he was a child, and there were children with no shoes. 'They all have shoes now. My mother says that children are better off since the war and all the babies look healthier since rationing and that pink stuff they get.'

'They do not have shoes. I have seen children without shoes.'

'I expect they just hadn't bothered to put them on. I often don't put my shoes on. I rather hate shoes if you want to know. I wish I lived in a place where I never had to wear them. If I lived in a warm place I'd never wear shoes.'

He paid no attention but just looked at me crossly. 'I should have thought that the daughter of F. J. Vye might have known about the conditions of the poor,' he said striding away again.

'Well, I suppose we *are* pretty poor,' I started . . .

'Not you,' he shouted over his shoulder. 'You're not poor. You're flaming rich. We're all flaming rich. Your family and mine don't know what poverty is.' He turned round with his eyes all fierce. 'Look, after this war there's going to be a change. Haven't you gathered that? No more rich men, no more Churchills, no more precious aristocrats. There's going to be a revolution. Hasn't anyone told you that? There's going to be a revolution.'

'Well there was a woman on the bus saying there'd be some changes.' (I was trying to calm him down.) 'What seemed to get her though was the bus conductress's hair.'

'Doesn't your father talk to you?'

'Not really. I know he doesn't like Churchill but mother and I think it might be jealousy. He does listen to all his speeches. You can't help being, well, I don't know . . . I go cold all up and down my back when he begins. Don't you?'

'That's not what I said.'

'Anyway, I don't know how you know what my father thinks.'

'I read him of course.'

'*Read* him?'

'Yes, his articles.'

'Oh – those,' I said. 'Good heavens.'

'What d'you mean? Haven't you read them?'

'Me? No. I haven't read them. Nor has mother. I know he writes them though. Yes – I know what you mean. He writes them for *The New Statesman* or something and mother says thank goodness because we couldn't manage otherwise. Not that they pay him all that much she says.'

'Didn't you know that they are absolutely brilliant?'

'Well I expect they are. He is brilliant. The archbishop came once and we all had to have lunch at the vicarage – absolutely freezing. The archbishop told Rowley – he was three – that father had a brilliant mind.'

'Not a Christian mind, thank goodness.'

'What?'

'I said, your father's not a Christian of course, thank

goodness.' He went striding on and then turned back with a gleam in his eye to where I was standing still. He did not look in the least like Rupert Brooke any more. His cheek-bones stuck out in a hectic sort of way.

'*What* did you say?'

'I said 'Your father's not a Christian of course'.'

'But of course he's a Christian. He gave up everything. He had a lovely job. We had a lovely house . . .'

'Oh yes, I dare say he's a saint, if there were such things that is – but he's not a Christian is he?'

'Well what is he then?'

'A Communist of course. Like Marx. Like Bernard Shaw. Like I am actually.'

'My father a Communist? My father?' Pictures went flying through my head of peasants on roads with their feet in bundles of rags and counts and princes and little children being lined up in front of guns, dead bodies on lamp posts, churches used as store-rooms and salt-mines. 'My father a Communist! You're mad! Communists don't – well, they don't believe in Jesus.'

'So what?'

'You mean – you think my father doesn't believe in Jesus?'

'Well of course.'

'You mean, you don't . . .'

'No of course not.'

I was absolutely stuck. I went silent and still, staring and staring at him, all heavy in the feet.

'Oh come on,' he said, looking over his shoulder into the

crowded trees. 'For crying out loud, you've surely met someone before who wasn't a Christian?'

There I stood.

'You mean you haven't? Oh come on!' He raised an eyebrow and the side of his nose. He was what my mother calls loving himself. 'Crikey, how innocent can you be? D'you think everyone's a Christian – bus conductresses and the kids you know at school? The kids in Cargo Fleet without any shoes? D'you think they go to church, holy, holy, holy?'

'Does – do your parents know?'

'I don't talk to my parents. They know how I feel of course about the way they live. They've stopped trying to make me join in things. They say it's my age which is what people always say. I can't stand the bourgeois.'

'What is bourgeois?'

'Well – oh just people like my parents.'

'Well,' I said, 'I know your mother's ghastly . . . Oh help!' His face all tipped back and proud had suddenly sort of flattened out. 'Oh help! I'm terribly sorry!'

It looked as if someone had thrown a plate at it. 'Oh lord, I'm sorry, I didn't mean to say that.'

'It's all right.'

'No – honestly, I shouldn't of. It was terrible. Actually I do admire your mother terribly. I mean – that wonderful party. I've never been to such a party. I don't know how she does it, in war-time. She must have been planning and saving up for weeks. She's so terribly, well so terribly clever you can see, and so strong and . . . oh heavens!'

'It's all right,' he said again. 'I think we ought to be getting back. You're catching the bus aren't you?'

'Yes of course,' I said very humbly, and we turned and went back along the hacked-up sugary path beside the wood, down the fields, through the churchyard, without even glancing at the plain which had made William the Conqueror swear, without seeing or saying anything at all. Mrs Fanshawe-Smithe stood at the garden door smiling like mad.

'Ah there you are dears! Solemn as two owls. A lovely walk? That's right. Jessica, you left a letter on the writing desk. Shall I drop it into the box?'

I suppose I wasn't normal or something but the flap of the letter seemed awfully loosely stuck down.

'Is she ill?' (Through the floor.)

'No, she's not ill.'

'Well, why's she in bed?'

'She's id a bood.'

'No, she's not, Rowley. Eat your porridge. Don't be rude.'

'I think he's right this time. She is in a mood.'

'A bad bood.'

'She's been in bed off and on for five days ever since the flipping party. What on earth happened? Has she written a thank you letter . . . I hope so. I like old Fan. He's a nice old guy. Good of them to ask her.'

'Yes of course she has, I posted it.'

'If you don't say fanks you gets no presents.'

'Can't you find out what's wrong with her?'

'Oh, leave her alone, Freddie. She's all right. There was that do when she came home.'

'What do?'

'I told you. She came in and there was something burning and I was out taking something or other to poor Mrs Baxter because she's started the flu and I'd just looked in at the church to see if that page's costume was there because we couldn't find it anywhere here and it was the dress rehearsal the next night, and while I was out Rowley – he was frightfully good really. I knew Jess would be back at any minute – after all the bus stops virtually at the door and I told him to sit and wait for her on the stairs and not *move* – Rowley had put wool everywhere.'

'I didn't hear about wool?'

'It was my string-alockment. Wound wound and wound the hallstand and the ballistairs.'

'He'd made a sort of spider's web everywhere so that you couldn't easily get to the kitchen to turn things off, and there were his toys here and there and he was doing something awful to that old doll.'

'Not Carol?'

'Yes, but it's absolutely years since she played with Carol. She's not looked at her for about seven years.'

'I tooken out her eyes. They was like a pair of little scales. They was joined together behind her nose. I had to break her head open. Jess got id a bood.'

'My word. My word! Poor old Jess! What happened?'

'She just went mad. I found her sobbing and howling in a

heap behind the hallstand – and the cabbage absolutely ruined. She was saying "It's all awful. I hate it. I'm going away. I'm leaving this mess. Look at the mess! Look at the smell!"'

'Boody! You can't see smells.'

'Sometimes you almost can. Poor old Jess.'

I put my head under the pillow because I've never been very sure about this floor business. You'd think they'd know I could hear through – they must know. After all, they shout through to each other if one's upstairs and one's in the kitchen. They just don't think. They just clean forget. It often seems very peculiar to me that my father has a brilliant mind.

When I came up for air he was saying, 'I'd like to get her something,' and mother was sounding pathetic and saying 'I thought she'd have such a lovely time. Perhaps it was that dress. I wish she'd had a better dress.' Cups and saucers clinked about but in a way that meant it would be some time before she got to the sink with them. Thump, she went, back in her chair. 'I *ought* to have got her a dress. I ought to have got her a dress somehow.'

'Oh come on. Dresses don't worry her.'

'Well they ought to. She's got nice long legs. She's thirteen.'

'Thirteen's a baby.'

'You don't have dresses on your legs. Was that the bell?'

(Yes it was. It's been ringing for hours.)

There were voices and the banging of a door, and a

moment's silence, and I was just beginning to think out how my parents had the time for the sort of pointless conversation they'd just been having; how they weren't so absolutely bored stiff with it that they ran out of the house and down the road screaming, or stepped side by side to the gas oven and laid down their heads in it – when I heard Ma say, very low and queer, 'Freddie, there's the most marvellous-looking boy in the hall. He wants to see Jess.

'Boy!'

'Yes. Hush. He just marched in. He just said, "I want to see Jessica." He's not very polite. I must say he's very handsome. My goodness . . .'

Father went thumping into the hall and I heard him booming, 'Hello. I'm Fred Vye. How do you do?' and then a hem and a hum and 'Ahem. How do you do . . . Sir.'

'You'd better come in. We're in the kitchen. Come and meet my wife and Rowley.'

'Hello.' (Mother's voice.)

'How do you do.' (Christian.)

Silence. After a time, 'You will be old Fan's son I expect?' 'Oh' – ahem, ahum, snuffle – 'Oh sorry. Yes, Christian.'

'You were asking for Jessica?'

'Well, actually, sir, it was you. It was you I had to see.'

'Oh yes?'

'It was about Middle-Class Morality.'

There was a really tremendous pause with only Rowley singing to his engines under the table, then father giving a great shout, 'Oh I see! Great Scot, I see. You mean Shaw?'

'I mean you, sir.'

'Notes on the Fabians?'

'Yessir.'

'Aha,' and they started talking.

HAVE NO FEAR. I am not going to go into it. Somehow I managed to get through all that other conversation about Rowley's string-alockment without dropping off to sleep, but this next one I couldn't and neither could you. I've only put this chapter in because it tells you quite a bit about Christian and how I felt when I got home. I could almost miss it out, really. I might yet. On and on they went. 'I don't quite agree sir, if you don't mind me saying so . . .' etc, etc, and mother, 'I'm so sorry, Christian, I must get on with the washing up . . .' and Rowley, 'I wanna go out now, please Mummy, *please* Mummy,' and father and Christian hearing nothing.

I'd been sitting bolt upright in bed for quite a long time and I lay down and put my head under the pillow and prayed, let me suffocate. Let me die.

14

Mrs Fanshawe's snow melted almost at once of course into brown mush and we had a dirty, warmish Christmas – a 'green' Christmas all the old ladies called it, coming out of church, but there didn't seem much that was green about it to me. 'We mustn't grumble,' they all said. 'Better than the snow. Yes, *very* nice, thank you. Quiet of course but that makes a nice change.' 'Well, there's not been much since mid-December,' the vicar said pausing with his hand on the wicket gate into the vicarage garden. The cold wind from the sea got under his long black cloak and blew it into a balloon. He looked as frail as leaves. 'Oh come, vicar,' Mrs Baxter started up, 'you wouldn't expect Jerry to come over at *Christmas*!' She was better from the 'flu and braced up very firmly in a sort of soldierly uniform with silver buttons. 'He'd have to be a very dirty dog to come at Christmas.' 'I expect you are right, I expect you are right.' He went tottering off across his great wet lawn which was all mangled up and turned into a vegetable allotment which didn't seem to be doing very well. Mrs Baxter said, 'The place is too much for him. They've billeted twenty-five air-men on him now you know. He's had to take up all his apples in the attic. Vicar, vicar! Your feet will get so wet. He needs goloshes or something.' She turned to me – I was hanging about waiting for father, and came up close to me and prodded me in the stomach. 'Time he went,' she said. 'Now, if we only had your – why, here he is. We were just saying what a quiet Christmas it has been, Mr Vye. Not that Jerry would come at Christmas of course.'

'And why not?'

'Why – the birthday of our Lord!'

'What is? December 25th? Rubbish, Mrs Baxter. Just a day they chose with a pin. More like March they think now, birth of Christ. Come on, Jess. Glad you're better, Mrs Baxter – blooming like a rose. Lovely weather. Only man is vile. Oh that woman!'

'She'll hear you, for goodness sake!'

'No she won't she's deaf as a post. Deaf as a fiddle-de-dee.'

'Is a fiddle-de-dee deaf?'

'Yes.' (We went on like this for a bit) 'By the way, you're going out this afternoon. Forgot to tell you.'

'Out?'

'Yes. With that character.'

'What character?'

'That Adonis. That Romeo. That fellow who can't stop talking about setting the world to rights.'

'Who? Not . . .'

'Yes – that Christian. I say he's got an unfortunate name hasn't he? Poor old thing. He'll change it before long to Will or Hasp or something. I think I'll call him Hasp.'

149

I said I'd never heard of Hasp and what did he mean, 'going out'?

'Hasp, I'll say to him, Hasp, when you're my age, before you're my age, when you're a bishop with your sons down for Charterhouse, when you've stopped thinking about morality and only about minutes . . .' He carried on like this until we were over the road and almost at home and I writhed and kicked the front door and said, 'Oh do shut up talking rubbish. You're not like a father. I don't understand what you're talking about.'

A wail came from the kitchen — Rowley getting too near the fat — and an exasperated cry from mother.

I said, 'If you want to know, Christian Fanshawe-Smithe says that you aren't a Christian. He says you're a Communist and everybody knows it. That's why he thinks you're so marvellous if you want to know. He doesn't like Christians that's why he likes you. He's a Communist. He says there's going to be a revolution. He says you're a . . .'

But as he removed his coat father had caught sight of himself in the hallstand and pulled down a piece of hair diagonally over his eyes and put two fingers under his nose and did a Sieg-Heil sign and screamed and shouted at himself (he's always in a good mood after Sung Eucharist). 'Who'm I?' he asked.

'Oh do shut up.'

He smoothed his hair and put on a melancholy hat that was hanging on the hallstand and picked up a fat umbrella and put on a dismal face, 'Who'm I now?'

'Mr Chamberlain, ha, ha, very funny.' Actually he was.

'Words, idle words, I know not what they mean,' he said. 'Now coom and get thi dinner. Communists aren't much of a hand at eating and I've an idea it's beef.'

Which it was though a queer shape and very small, and then a tin of peaches from South Africa – Yellow Cling, as good as Christmas. I went upstairs and put on my new jersey knitted by one of father's admirers for me for a Christmas present. Not bad. Rather a ghastly green. I did my hair and wished for some silk stockings instead of lisle, though thank goodness I had a pair without darns in. I heard the bell and felt absolutely terrible. I heard Ma asking him if he'd like some coffee. I heard him say that we really ought to be going as we were catching the twenty-two past the hour. I came slinking into the kitchen feeling sick and ugly and he didn't even turn round.

Mother said, 'Oh are you thinking . . . are you going to High Thwaite? Jessica's father didn't say. He just said he'd seen you when he was at High Thwaite for the Diocesan Meeting.'

'He said it would be all right,' said Christian. Father came into the room and Christian turned brick red and smiled. 'You did say, sir . . .'

'Oh yes, of course,' said father. 'Hello Hasp – um, Christian. Perfectly all right.'

I said, 'For goodness sake!'

'Where are you taking her?'

'To the slums. I thought we might go and see something of the slums.'

'I beg – I beg your pardon?'

'She said she'd never seen the slums.'

'Oh I see. What . . . slums are those?'

'Oh just round about. Teesside generally.'

'Teesside,' mother said. 'Oh dear! Of course, we hardly ever go there now. When we first came they had a Father Christmas in Binns at Shields East. It's funny. I never really think of it as slums. I expect it's living so near.'

'There aren't slums near *Binns*,' he said earnestly, 'not near the shops. I mean under the bridge, down by the docks, in among the back-to-back houses.'

'No,' said Ma, very definitely. 'No, I'm sorry, Christian. Jess is not going round Shields East docks on a Sunday afternoon,' and she dried her hands on a tea-cloth she had been absent-mindedly holding and went off into the kitchen.

'It'll be all right, Katie,' father shouted. 'They won't be allowed anywhere dangerous. I doubt,' he dropped a hand on Christian's shoulder, 'whether you will be allowed near the docks at all.'

'May I show her the slum housing areas then?'

'No harm in that. I'm not sure exactly where they are.'

'Freddie, there are *Lascars* there!' she shouted from the kitchen.

'No, no – not there, love. There are Lascars and all sorts round the docks, but I tell you they won't be allowed in there.'

'Well there are some terrible people in Shields East . . .'

'There are terrible people everywhere.'

'There I cannot agree with you,' said Christian. Father glittered and gleamed.

'All right then,' he said, 'off you go, but I expect her back by six o'clock and when I say six o'clock I mean six o'clock, because it will be dark.'

'I don't like it,' called mother.

'I wanna go, I wanna go,' Rowley cried and stretched his arms out to me in the most loving way, 'I wanna go with Jessica.'

Father picked him up and went with us to the door. 'No – you stay here, it's your rest time. Can't cosset them for ever,' I heard him say and mother called back, 'She's far too young. She's far too young to be going out with boys.'

We took a bus into the town from the stop outside our house and it went whirling along very fast as it was nearly empty – the driver wanting to get home for his Sunday dinner – and got off it at the town clock and set off for the station. Christian went loping ahead like a giraffe, head forward, and me trotting behind. We didn't speak. I saw Dottie Hobson and Cissie Comberbach coming out as we got to the booking office. Dottie must be having Cissie over for tea-and-stay-the-night and gone to meet her. They both stopped and stared at Christian with their mouths open but I only had time to wave and fly on. At the little window Christian asked for two return Shields East and I thought, then it's real. He's paying. I'm going out with him.

The ticket office man said, 'Two? You mean one-er-alf. Jessica's not fourteen.' He's one of the sidesmen. 'One and a half, then,' said Christian not moving a muscle, 'Return.' (So he was coming back! He was bringing me right back.

However would he get back to High Thwaite? He was seeing me right home!!) I felt very happy indeed all of a sudden and I followed him along the platform and over the bridge. I thought I heard the sidesman shout something at me from his window, but I was running to catch up.

Half way over the wooden bridge we saw the train was in ready to go – it must have been the one Cissie had got off from Cleveland Spa. She must have come in on a bus to Cleveland Spa from the farm, changing at Brotton or Skinningrove or somewhere. What a faff-on. I didn't even know she got on with Dottie. She worms herself in everywhere. Whatever would they do with themselves all afternoon? Play Beetle most likely or Marriage Consequences.

The carriage was full of men going on the Sunday shift in dungarees under their hard coats, each with a tea can and tin box. They were all shaved and clean, their faces awake, not like they would be coming back in the early morning, sleeping, rocking about, jaws hanging and dirty. When we got to Marsh Halt a few got out and a great many more got in. They all looked at Christian and he looked straight ahead of him. One of them said something to the man next to him and they both laughed and settled down for a steady examination of him, but not unkind. One of them saw me watching and gave me a wag of the head sideways and a wink. A voice in my head said, 'I love every greasy, dirty, sulky wrinkle, every button on his unclean waistcoat.' Who'd said it? Christian? Was it this gift I have, reading his mind? I looked at him but somehow it didn't seem likely. He was looking really rather proud and stately. 'Was it myself thought that? Do I?' Then I remembered — it was in Miss Philemon's copy of Rupert Brooke. It was one of his letters to someone or other. He was saying how he loved everything just for being there. He loved every greasy button. He was feeling very happy at the time.

I looked steadily at the workman opposite and thought, 'I am feeling very happy too. Yes — I do. I do love him. I love everything about him. I love everything. I love everyone. Oh heavens!' Christian was holding my hand!

'Every greasy button . . . Every . . . I love . . .' and I stared very hard at the workman who began to shift about and look uneasy.

Holding my hand!

The man who had wagged his head before and hadn't got out at Marsh Halt caught my eye and wagged his head and winked again. 'He's seen,' I thought. 'Oh heavens! My hand's getting wet! It's getting wet. Oh goodness,' and I tried to pull it away, but Christian hung on harder. 'I shall die,' I thought. 'This is the happiest day of my life. I shall never, never be happier than this. Oh gosh, my hand is getting terrible.'

The train stopped and incredibly — absolutely incredibly — it was Shields East already. When had we stopped at all the other stations? I'd meant to look at the steelworks — the train went right through the middle of them. You could look out on your left and see the steelworks smoking and blazing and on your right at the long ridges of the hills. To the left is what man made, to the right is what God made, the vicar had said in one of his wandery sermons once. I hadn't seen any of it. And Christian hadn't mentioned any of it either. And we were here and he let go my hand and wiped his own on his trousers. Oh how awful! How awful. It wasn't fair. My other one wasn't at all sticky. I suppose it couldn't have been *his* hand that was wet? Could it be . . .

The workmen were getting out fairly slowly, collecting their gas masks off the rack above them and their bait boxes. The one who had wagged his head and winked was last. As he got down on to the platform he turned back and leaned in, tapping me sharply on the knee. 'Now then!' he said. 'Think on. Siren's gone. Think on, that's all.'

Christian heard him and called, 'Hi – did you say the siren?' but the man was off through the barrier.

'That's right,' said the ticket collector. 'Siren all right. False alarm most likely. Can't see 'im bothering 'isself of a Sunday afternoon. Where 'yer off then?'

'Oh – just round the streets,' said Christian.

'Well, think on. We've 'ad 'im in daylight afore. Tha never knows.'

At the station entrance Christian looked up at the sky. It was bright and windy, clean blue and white above the heavy black buildings.

'It's faired-up,' I said.

'Mmmm. I say, I think we'd better go back . . .'

'Go *back*! Oh no! No, Christian, no.'

'I think we should. It just might be a raid. I can't think so really – there's not been one for ages and they hardly ever come in daylight, but they just might.'

'Oh no, Christian, no, no, no. You mean go back home?'

(The house with them all resting? Dead, dreadful Sunday afternoon. The smell of the Sunday gravy? And if they read this I don't care.) 'It's absolutely quiet. The all-clear will go in a minute. It's nothing at all.'

'I've not been in a raid,' he said. 'At school it's right in the country. We've heard Liverpool in the distance but it's fifty miles away.'

I said, 'Oh, they're nothing. Noisy, that's all. Oh *please*. Please – I do want to see the slums. *Please* don't let's!'

There was nobody about at all in the bright, quiet afternoon just the sun shining and a group of lads in black suits and long white silk scarves for Sunday, talking on a corner and making smaller and smaller circles on their bikes.

'It'll be a false alarm,' he said at last. 'Come on.'

We walked to the bridge that led over to the docks and went under it, but great iron gates had gone up since Christian was last there, with No Admittance signs. We turned back and passed the station again and one of the lads shouted at Christian – something about his hair keeping him warm. Then we turned left, and right, then left again and into a long drab dreary street that seemed to go on for ever, everywhere bolted and barred up. We turned off this street, too, and came to another. It had flat, rectangular little slabs all over the road and the little houses were of plum-coloured brick with black cement between them, very hideous. The window-ledges were dirty yellow and there were dirty dark net curtains in the windows with blackened plants in pots in between, or a pot-alsatian or a china child holding its dress out on either side and smirking into the street. Off this street led other streets of even poorer-looking houses. At the end of each of these was the railway embankment going up to the railway line and this was covered in tin cans and broken fencing and ashes and rubbish. We stood on the corner of one of these – Dunedin Street it said on a painted black and white board – and looked down it. Two children were sitting on a doorstep, a thin cat was walking across the little brick cobbles and a hollow-eyed man was leaning against a door-post. It was very quiet – even the children seemed not to be talking. Only now and then the man coughed and spat into the road, then settled back against the door-post and watched us. Some of the windows in the street were boarded up. There were sandbags outside one house, bursting and filthy, and barbed-wire round the door of an empty one that seemed to be falling down. There was a sour smell about.

'There,' said Christian. 'That's what I mean.'

'Is it a slum?'

'Well – what do you think?'

'Yes. Well, yes. I suppose it is a slum. It's pretty awful.'

'*Pretty* awful?'

'Yes – I suppose so. Somehow I thought it was going to be worse.'

'Could it be worse?'

'Well, I think I expected green slime or something. Just shacks and green slime. I mean I haven't seen anywhere worse exactly . . . But if they planted a few trees . . . If it was all painted white, and it was in Africa or somewhere and they had bright-coloured clothes.'

'Why are you trying to make the best of it?' He turned on me and absolutely blazed. 'What's the matter with you? This is hell isn't it?' The man coughed and spat and settled back to watch again.

'Hell!' cried Christian, 'Hell, hell, hell. I want to get rid of all this. I want to knock it down. Don't you see, it's got to be destroyed?' and he raised his terrific long arms up above his head. 'It must be destroyed!' he cried and the man straightened up and pointed at the sky with a look of utter unbelief on his face.

'Run!' we heard him cry. 'You kids – run will yer,' and the whole sky was torn apart in the crash that answered him and was followed by a great avalanche of falling brick.

The guns took over from it. They were like giants who had been lying waiting. '*Now* we'll get you,' they seemed to say. They spoke out from behind the houses from just over the railway – from just behind Dunedin Street. Something tremendous thundered from the docks and the world disappeared in yellow dust.

When I opened my eyes I was right down the street by myself lying on the pavement and looking at a broken china alsatian. There was glass everywhere. I felt about and found I was near the doorstep of one of the houses. The door had blown inwards and there was someone lying still in the passage just inside. 'Where's Christian?' I thought – I think I said it, 'Oh goodness! Where's Christian?' The dark bundle in the passage got up and began crawling towards me. It wasn't Christian but the man who had been coughing. We looked at each other on our hands and knees about a foot from the ground for what seemed a very long time. Then the man turned his head away and began to cough again, very horribly, until he was tired of it. He sat back on his haunches and leaned back against the wall just inside the door. 'Aye-oop!' he said.

I blinked. 'Aye-oop now. We'd best go inside and see what's tooken moother.'

'What?'

'Aye-oop now. That's a daisy. 'Ere we are. Now then.' He was heaving me up and pushing me along the passage as he spoke and into a front room where a man was cowering in a corner with his back to the room like a shell and the most enormous woman I had ever seen was bulging back in a battered arm-chair. She had no legs and she was roaring with laughter.

I began to shake. For the first time since I had opened my eyes after the bomb – it must have been a bomb. That terrible avalanche, that dreadful wind – for the first time I began to be afraid. 'She has no legs. She has no legs,' I heard myself saying. I saw the little old man shaking his head back across the room, and back on to his chair. 'No legs. No legs.'

They must have been blown off. I found myself looking round the room for the legs.

'Eeeeeeh, Ernie lad, bring 'er. Bring 'er 'ere,' said the woman. 'Now then! Now then! Thast *all* right. Hush then. Hush lass thast all right.'

(No legs. No legs.)

'I cannot come to thee,' said the great woman, 'I cannot

come. I's no legs. Never for years. Not sin a bairn. There lass, there. Git kettle on now, Ern lad. Hush lass, hush. She's afeared . . .'

I went over to the woman who took my hand and I sat on the fender. Ern went out and could be heard filling the kettle. (So they did have water. It wasn't hell. I'd tell Christian. Oh where was Christian?)

''Ere's thy brother,' called Ern and Christian came tumbling in. He was very dirty and had cut his face. His coat was torn. 'Get help!' he shouted. 'Quick – get help. There's houses down and people trapped. Down the street. Quick!' He looked round the room, dazed at the sight of the little old man over the fire, the fat woman leaning back in her chair holding my hand and patting the top of it and the noise of tea cups outside.

'There's people *trapped*!'

'It's all right, they're 'ere,' said Ern coming in with some thick cups. People began to run down Dunedin Street, one blowing a whistle. Ambulance bells began to ring, getting nearer. Fire engines arrived and there were shouts, and children crying.

'I'll just . . .' Christian made for the door.

'Nay – siddown,' said Ern. 'Drink thy tea.' He began drinking his own, slapping his lips.

'Nowt but kids,' said the old man. 'Only kids. Of a Sunday afternoon. Whatyer 'ere for of a Sunday afternoon?'

The fat woman began to laugh again. She laughed by pulling her fat chin into her neck and closing her eyes and baring her teeth for a while before the sound began to come out in a long tight wheeze. 'Eeeeeh!' she said, her eyes streaming, "'Ere's Ern int passage on 'is 'ands and knees and 'eres father with 'is face int corner and all on us awaitin' fort end oft world. Topsy turvy, topsy turvy! And on a Sunday afternoon! Who'd of thought it on a Sunday afternoon?'

'It'd be a tip and run,' said the old man. 'That's what it'd be a tip and run. Funny just one bang and right on Dunedin Street. Why did it have to be Dunedin Street? Quiet god-fearing folk like us,' he grumbled.

'God-fearing folk!' laughed the woman still patting and patting my hand and wheezing with laughter. 'Quiet god-fearing folk! Git away, father! Drink thy beer. Eeh look – it's never spilt! It's ont mantelshelf and never spilt!'

'Hoses!' cried a man running past the window. 'Fetch hoses.'

'Nay – I's no taste for beer,' said the old man, 'at present.'

Ern came in off the street. 'It's fifty-three,' he said. 'It's fifty-three downt other end. It's Gadsby's. I seed it,' he said, 'I seed it with me own eyes.'

'What?' said Christian.

'I seed it – I seed t'aeroplane with its swastikas ont. I seed it up above!'

'Eeeeh, Ern, thast daft!' laughed the woman.

'I tell yer I seed it!' He seemed furious that such a thing should ever be seen. At night he could understand it. But in the daytime it was disgusting. 'Just as he lifts his arms, this lad, I seed it. I seed the man inside it.'

'He'd be a German likely,' said the old man. The old woman roared with laughter.

'I'm a Peterborough man,' said the old man. 'I'm from Peterborough. It's a grand place Peterborough. We should of stayed in Peterborough.'

'He was a bloody German,' shouted Ern. Things were slowly dawning on him. 'A bloody German. I seed his bloody face!'

'Dearie me!' laughed the woman.

'Didst a know, lass,' said the old man, 'as it were a Peterborough man as invented the zip fastener?' I thought, 'They're mad.'

In the street somebody shouted, 'Outside, OUTside. Everybody outside.' and Christian went to the door. 'They're getting everybody out,' he said. 'There's a big crowd. They're putting ropes up. Come on Jess, we can go.'

'Nay,' said the woman, 't'lass must sit a bit. Let her sit a bit.'

'We've got to go.'

'Where wilt tha go?'

'Home,' said Christian. 'On the train. Quick, Jess.'

'There'll be no train I doubt.'

'Yes there will. Come on, Jess, quick. They'll stop us if we don't go now. They'll start putting us in an ambulance or something.'

'Sit a bit,' said the woman. 'They can't put us out. They can't get me out no-how. It teks a crane to shift me,' and she leaned back and began the long wheeze and laugh. 'Sit a bit longer,' she said.

But we went. We fled. Over hosepipes, past firemen,
A.R.P.'s, home-guards, crowds of sightseers. Someone
shouted, ''Ere! Names and addresses now,' but we were off,
flying through the streets to the station.

'Station's shut,' said a man. 'Roof's down. Watcht glass.'

'Git out,' screamed someone else. 'D'yer want yer
deaths? There'll be no trains today.'

Christian looked lost and said, 'What shall we do?'

'There'll be buses.' I said. 'We'll get a bus. Where's the
bus station?'

'I don't know.'

We asked and at last we found it – six long cement platforms with railings and not a bus in sight. Nobody in sight.
A desert.

'It's Sunday afternoon. There's hardly a single bus on a
Sunday.'

'Anyway, we'd better ring up home.'

I said we weren't on the phone. I supposed I could ring
the vicar.

'I'll ring High Thwaite,' he said. 'Or maybe I'd better
thumb a lift to Guisborough and get a bus or another lift
from there. Or walk. But there's you.'

'Me?'

'Yes, what're you going to do?'

'Oh – I. I'll be all right. I suppose if I ring the vicarage
someone might come. The vicar's so deaf though and the
housekeeper's not there on Sunday afternoon.'

A bus suddenly appeared and we ran across to see what it
was. It went to Thwaite Lane End.

'Quick, get in,' I said.

'I can't just leave you.'

'Yes, you can – quick get in. It'll be the last today. I'll be all right.'

He got in slowly and some more people appeared from somewhere and joined him. Everyone was exclaiming about the bomb. 'It was Dunedin Street,' someone said. 'Two children killed there.' 'Two? Nay – I heard five.'

I said, 'Don't hang about. Go on. Go and sit down,' and I walked away over to the other side of the bus station to the platforms where I thought we used to catch the buses home when we came up to Binns. When his bus went out everywhere was quite empty. There was a bit of newspaper blowing about from platform to platform, very slowly in the wind, and I watched and could hear it scraping right over the other side. I held on to the fat iron railing and thought for a long time. I supposed the raid was over though I'd heard no all clear, but then I hadn't heard the siren either. It felt over. The aeroplane must be far away by now, with the German sitting inside it. I wondered if he had actually seen Christian and me. He must have been aiming at the docks or something and had not been a very good shot.

'No legs,' I thought. I thought of the fat woman and the old man and the man who had invented the zip fastener. What is it that I am trying not to think? I thought of Christian sitting in the bus, looking straight forward, not waving as it bowled away.

'He left me,' I said. 'He didn't even ask if I'd any money to get home.

'Dear God,' I said, 'thank you very much for not letting me be killed in Dunedin Street, and please help me to get home.'

The piece of paper jumped in the air and flattened itself against some railings, and with a roar a bus came racing round the corner with the Cleveland number on the front. Sitting inside it all alone was Miss Philemon.

15

The following morning my mother got the washing started early because the vicar's cook had asked to have Rowley for the day. He and father had gone off at eight-thirty with dinky cars and some of the gas-piping Rowley likes and a few big nails. Father said he would go on to take the nine o'clock as it was Holy Innocents and then do the hospital visiting. Mother said she was sorry but the Holy Innocents would have to get on without her. She'd got more washing than she'd had for ages what with Christmas and the Nativity Play.

By half past nine she had got most of the big wash done, the handkerchiefs boiling and a bowl of things soaking on the kitchen floor when she remembered the fish that had been in the house since Saturday and was asking for attention as father had noticed at breakfast. Since there was no fat to fry it in it had to be boiled, so she dropped it into cold water. It Swam flabbily down to the bottom (I wasn't there. I'm making this part up. I'd swear to every word though) and in about ten minutes it was steaming away beside the handkerchiefs. She let down the ceiling airer to hang up the smalls indoors because it was beginning to sleet outside. 'But they'll smell of fish,' she said – (she always does). 'They'll have to be hung out in the end to get rid of it. Not that it ever really does get rid of it. Not till they're washed again. Was that the bell?' She listened and said, 'No, thank goodness. I certainly don't want anybody this morning.'

She hauled up the airer and pushed her hair out of her eyes. 'My *hair* smells of fish. Horrible.' There was a very long peal on the bell. 'I knew it,' she said and opened the front door throwing her apron down beside the hallstand at the same time. Mrs Fanshawe-Smithe was on the step.

'My dear!' (Something like this.)

'Oh.' She put her wet hands behind her and then brought them out again and her face became all over knobs. 'Oh, hello.'

'My dear!' She came right in without being asked and stood in the passage. 'My dear, I am Barbara Fanshawe-Smithe. You are Kate Vye. How do you do?'

'Do come in.' Ma looked helplessly about. Since she was in, it was a silly thing to say. 'Come into the – the parish store-room.

'My dear, I shouldn't dream of it. Let me come into the *kitchen*. I knew you'd be busy. Now I'll be really cross if you stop what you're doing.'

'I'd love to stop what I'm doing. Come into the parish room and I'll make some coffee,' and she nodded and smiled and Mrs F-S had to go in and sit herself down on the window seat and Mother on a heap of stuff on the piano stool, thinking most likely (because she would) that she was winning and also thank heavens; and also that she was going to force her to have coffee because the fish needed turning down fast.

'Now, you are going to have some coffee,' she said and Mrs F-S drew off her gloves and said that that would be very nice.

'Second round to me,' thought mother. 'Whatever does Freddie mean? She's a duck. She looks like a cook. I'm not afraid of her. Men are queer,' and she flew round the kitchen turning things off and put her foot in a bowl of socks. She scratched some Nescafé out of the bottom of the tin we got at Christmas and sliced up some Christmas cake, getting dryish, dug out a tray, dried her foot, poured the boiling water into the cups and came swanning back, smiling. 'Here we are. I've got some real sugar, too. Lovely to stop for coffee.'

Mrs F-S took her cup and stirred it and looked up with her charming smile. 'How is she?' she asked. 'How is Jessica?'

'Jessica? Oh she's quite well, thank you. She's at church I think doing the hymn boards and then she's going to see a school friend. I haven't really seen her this morning.'

'She's not injured? She's not hurt at all? My dear I'm so glad.'

'Injured? But why ever . . .'

'I'm afraid poor Christian is in bed.'

'Christian . . .'

'My dear, you mean you don't know?'

'Don't know?'

'About the raid. My dear, the raid. They were in Dunedin Street.'

Ma began to blush like mad with fright. She heard her cup rattle on the saucer. 'In it?' she said. 'In it? Oh no, Mrs — er. No they weren't, I'm sure they weren't.'

'I'm afraid they were. Christian told me. He never tells us anything so I know that it's true. He is very badly shaken, Mrs Vye. He walked straight into the library, white as a ghost and said, "We were bombed. We were in Dunedin Street. It was bombed."'

'But — they *can't* have been. I mean Jessica tells us everything' (Ha!) 'We were terribly anxious as a matter of fact. It was a horrible afternoon. I knew they'd gone to Shields East. We were both frightened but my — my hus — Freddie said being frightened would not help and we must just wait. And when we heard her open the door at a quarter to six we just looked at each other and thought thank God. And he said, "Now don't show you've been worried. Don't let her think we're treating her like a baby." We didn't know there'd been any bombing then.'

'I see.'

'She *can't* have been in Dunedin Street. There was a direct hit there,' and Ma began to shake (I hope). 'People were killed.'

'But I'm afraid they were. Christian talked and talked about it. We couldn't stop him. He hasn't opened his mouth for weeks — it's his age of course. He's only fourteen though he looks so much older. They were taken in by some very good sort of people — a woman with no legs and a T.B.-sounding man. My husband is talking of going to find them and rewarding them in some way. But I expect they've all been evacuated by now.'

'But she *couldn't* have been! She just called, "I'm back" and went up to her room. She seemed asleep when I took her supper up. She didn't want any breakfast this morning – oh goodness! I wonder if she's all right.'

'I wonder.'

'I – I must go and find her.' Ma stood up. 'I must go at once.'

'That would be wise.'

Ma rushed out and began battling with the coats on the hallstand.

'My dear, don't worry.' She came up behind. 'You have nothing to reproach yourself with. It's not as if you *knew* there was going to be a raid.'

Ma put her frizzy head into the coats and said, 'We did. oh we did. The siren went two minutes after they left the house. I said to Freddie, go after them and he went to the station. On his bicycle. But the sidesman – he's in the ticket office – said the train had just left. He said he shouted at them to say there was a siren but they didn't listen.'

'I see. Well . . .'

'I must go to church and find her. I must go now.'

'I will come with you.'

'There's no need. I think I'd better see her on her own. If you were there she might be . . .'

'Nonsense, there's nothing alarming about me' (charming laugh). 'By the way, did you know Christian had been seeing Jessica – I mean *before* this escapade?'

'*Seeing* her? Yes of course, he came the day after the party. Actually I think it was more to see my husband than Jess. They, they . . .

'Oh yes, I can see that might be so. Has he taken her out very much? Made dates with her?'

'Dates? Goodness, no!'

'One simply doesn't know with one's children does one? Christian has simply never noticed a girl before. Most extraordinary. Girls of course are so much more mature . . .' (Stink-bomb, stink-bomb, filth-woman, drains.) 'I think, you know that it is wise just to check up with the parents of one's children's friends, do you?'

'All I think is that we should see that they're all right now.'

'It's so odd you didn't notice something.'

'It's not odd at all. Jessica's not in our pockets. I don't spy on her. I wouldn't dream of checking up with the parents of her friends what she was up to. They're not six-year-olds.'

'But my dear, of course I didn't mean *tell* the children one was checking up.'

'Oh I know Freddie wouldn't keep things like that from her. He's honest. He'd say it was wrong. If he got in touch with you to see if you agreed that Christian should take Jessica out, I know he would tell Jessica he was going to. But he never *would* ask. We know everything about each other in this house. We don't go in for spying.'

'So odd of her, then, not to tell you about the air-raid.'

I was sitting in the front pew in the side aisle with the red hymn board across my knees. Numbers were spread out along the pew in front of me and I had the number box at the side of me. I was looking at the pulpit as they came in. I'd expected something to happen soon and I didn't look round.

'Jess,' hissed mother and there was a commotion in the pulpit because Florence Bone was up there being someone from her opera. She bobbed down out of sight.

'Jess, whatever are you doing?'

'Nothing.'

'Who's that up there?'

'Who's what?'

'I saw someone up in the pulpit.'

'It was the Holy Ghost.'

'Jess!!!!!'

Florence came awkwardly down the steps. 'It's only me,' she said.

'Are you dusting or something?'

'No.'

'We're doing plays.' I pretended I'd just seen Mrs F-S and I said, 'Oh hello.' I sounded as if she was just anyone — just an equal — and because of this gift I have I saw that there was nothing I could have done to annoy her more. She would never, ever, forget the way I'd said it. Oh goody and hurray.

'Jess, Mrs Fanshawe has told me something very upsetting about yesterday. Can you come home, dear? Come home with us at once.'

'We're busy with plays.'

'Well stop being busy with plays.'

'No thanks.'

'That will do, Jess, it's about the – raid. I hear you were in the raid. Jess, I haven't even *seen* you since. Christian is ill.'

'I can't come now,' I said. 'We're doing something. We've just thought of something.'

'I'm going Jess, anyway,' said Florence. 'It's nothing important. See you tomorrow.'

'Christian is very shocked. Dear, I must see if you're all right. He's quite ill.'

'Ill, is he,' I said and I began to pile up the numbers carefully in stacks, fives on top of fives, and then slot them into the box. I got up and wandered to the nearest pillar and stood on a pew and began to make dabs at the hook with the empty board, slap, slap. I kept on missing. 'I'm sorry, I can't come,' I said, 'I'm going to stay here a bit.'

'But Jess!' She came up close and started begging. She whispered, 'Mrs Thing has come all the way from High Thwaite to see if you are all right.'

'I am all right,' I said, watching Mrs Fanshawe in the shadows.

'You must come home.'

'I'm coming soon.'

'I'll go home and get Daddy if you don't come this minute.'

I saw with interest that she was nearly crying and that her hands were clenched in the pockets of her beastly old coat and that she was losing face in front of Mrs F-S and that she called father Daddy. For an absolute second I nearly howled. I nearly started. However I said, 'Sorry, but I'm all right. Yesterday was nothing at all. It seemed to upset Christian. I'm sorry I couldn't see him home. My bus came in.'

There was nothing for it – I'm big. They couldn't drag me. They had to go. Florence had already gone and I was left all alone by the pew and just as they were shutting the door I said, loud and clear and most peculiar, 'GOOD RID-DANCE TO BAD RUBBISH.'

I got down and slid the lid on the number box and went off to the vestry and put it away. I came back through the chancel and sat down a minute at the organ and pulled out a few china knobs. Then I put my head down on the keys and all of a sudden I was right up above the rood screen looking down and I saw myself as I had done before in Miss Philemon's flat, very small and crumpled with my face pressed against the keys and my shoulders narrow and my hair parted down the back in two hunks. I saw the thick dust on the top of the wood carving of the rood screen and the cobwebs between Christ's hand and the scroll on the top of the cross which I'd never seen from below. 'What a poor small body I have,' I thought and was immediately back in it. I got up and went home. 'Oh *fish*,' I thought. 'Fish on top of everything else. I'm going to bed.'

'I don't want any dinner,' I shouted and went to my bed-room and sat at my desk. There was a bright blue exercise book on it. The white sleet that had settled on the shelter roof opposite reflected into the room and shone on the blue book. 'Ill,' I thought. 'And in bed I wouldn't wonder. Trays brought up!' I looked out at the snow and then pulled the blue book towards me and opened it and wrote a poem in it.

I wrote it straight out until it was finished and then got up and went looking for blotting paper under some comics. I blotted it and read it through and put in some commas and changed a word. Then I read it through again and sat down and wrote '*The Maniac*' at the top, underlined that, and blotted it and shut the book. Then I went to bed and slept till tea-time.

When I heard Rowley's coming-home voice, and father, I knew the day was nearly over. I heard mother call them into the kitchen and the whole tale retold and the argument grow louder – 'No I *haven't* been up to see her,' etc. – and in the end mother starting to cry and Rowley starting to hammer at the table-end because it was supper-time, and the coal being shot on to the fire and the sound of the blackouts being put up and I sat up in bed in the dark.

'I'll have to go down and say I'm sorry I suppose,' I thought. 'I will go soon. Poor mother. I must have been a bit mad or something. And Mrs Fanshawe-Smithe! Did I dream that? I'm sure I saw her with mother in church. I can't have! I can't have! And being up in the rafters in the chancel. That cobweb. I've been dreaming.

'That's it, I've been dreaming. I've been dreaming ever since Dunedin Street. Perhaps I got a blow on the head. With that pot dog I wouldn't wonder. Well, I'd better go down and see what's up. I feel terribly happy for some reason. I wonder if I'm going really mad? They say you go mad about my age sometimes!' I thought of Christian being ill and wondered how I knew. I thought of him riding away in the bus not looking at me. I thought of in the train when

I'd suddenly felt him holding my hand. I remembered being thrilled by that and my inside twisting around. I didn't feel thrilled now, but I felt terribly happy. Very peculiar.

I got out of bed and saw the blue exercise book and remembered the poem. I went over and read it and stood looking at it for a long time and knew why I felt happy. There was nothing in it I wanted to change.

Part III

The Poem

16

The doctor was looking down and there were some other people in the room. The black-out had been put up and the reading lamp was on, with a shade over it and standing on the floor. The doctor was saying, 'Well, she's awake now anyway.'

He got hold of my chin and moved it kindly from side to side. On the whole I don't get on very well with doctors. You can't get near them somehow. They always look afraid you're going to start talking. Ours is always sort of poised in doorways looking at his watch. He wasn't today though.

'Well, young lady,' he said (they have this soppy way of talking to you, too). 'What's all this then?'

I stared.

'Been in the thick of it, eh?'

I half sat up on my elbows and said I was just going down for tea. I must have got back into bed.

'Lie down,' he said, 'and let's look you over.'

'It was yesterday,' said Rowley's voice somewhere, 'Jessica's slept all today and yesterday.'

'What!'

'*That's* it. Now then lean forward and let's hear the back. That's it –'

'Have I been asleep?'

'That's it. Legs now. That hurt? Good. Yes, since yesterday. Your father and mother thought I'd better come and see you when you hadn't woken up by this afternoon. Thought you might have had a bang on the head. Can't see much wrong with you though. Any aches and pains?'

I thought about it and said, no I felt nice.

'That's it. No headaches? Anything hit you?'

'No, I don't think so. Only an alsatian.'

'*I* see. Well, back to sleep. I'll come and see you tomorrow.'

He went out with father and mother began to fuss round the room, shaking a thermometer and bringing a jug of water, tidying the desk. Rowley rested his chin on the bed and made a long scream like a bomb. 'Hush, Rowley, for goodness sake!' She looked at me pretending she wasn't as she tucked the sheets in.

I said, 'It's all right. Is there a blue book on that desk – an exercise book? Yes, that one. Can I have it?'

'I don't think you ought to do any homework yet.' Ma hovered.

'It's all right.' I put the book under my pillow and because she was so terribly on the hop I said, 'Sorry, Ma,' and went back to sleep.

Much later on I woke up again and found they'd moved the reading lamp – still shaded! – to the mantelpiece and father was sitting by the gas fire which wasn't lit, shrouded up in blankets and reading the Bible. I felt it was a queer time of night. It was utterly quiet. I was lovely and warm and just lay there for a bit.

Over the fireplace there was a picture of Jesus as a boy with curly yellow hair, holding out his hands above a lot of rabbits and I said, 'I say, can you take that picture down?' listening to myself like a stranger. Most queer.

'What?' he said. 'This? All right. Something wrong with it?'

'Yes.'

He lifted it down and said, 'Hmm, yes. I see what you mean. How long has this been here?'

'Always I think. Auntie Nellie gave it to me when I was born.'

'Goodbye,' he said shoving it under the bed. 'How are you?'

I only just heard him though because I was falling asleep again, and when I woke next there was daylight coming through the cracks.

Rowley was bouncing steadily in his bed across the passage which meant it must be after a quarter to six and father was now asleep in the chair with the clean square above him on the wall where the picture had been and a dreadful mess of blankets and papers all round him. His shoes were off and his feet were stuck into a corner of the bookcase and the Bible was open face down on his chest.

'Hello,' I said.

He woke up and the Bible fell off but he caught it and smoothed out the pages very carefully and picked up the blue ribbon marker with the tips of his fingers and smoothed it in its place before he shut the book.

'What?'

'Nothing. I'm terribly hungry. I'm absolutely ravening.'

'Shall I cook some sausages?'

'Are there some?'

'Yes, I got some from old Slatford. He says he's sorry you're ill.'

'I'm not ill. I'm just so hungry.'

'All right I'm off. Where's my flaming shoes.'

'You shouldn't swear if you're a parson.'

'Not swearing, flaming shoes. Rather holy, come to think of it, flaming shoes. Jacob's ladder. "With twain he covered his face and with twain he covered his feet and with twain he did fly." Isaiah.'

'That wasn't shoes. You can't cover your face with shoes. It was wings.'

'Where's my flaming wings then?' He burrowed about knocking things over, dregs of tea, a waste paper basket — 'If I grew some flaming wings there'd be a stir. I wonder what Mrs Baxter would say?'

I said that I was glad that he was not a Communist, and he said that he was glad that I was glad.

My father and I sometimes go on like this.

By lunchtime I was all right and the next day fine.

'That's the ticket,' said the doctor. 'No bones broken, no harm done. When does school start, Mrs Vye?'

'Tomorrow.'

I said, 'Oh Lord!'

'Well — you know there's really no reason why she shouldn't go. Back to the grind, eh? Best thing possible — the common round and all that. She's quite all right. Not talking about alsatians any more, eh?'

'I *was* hit by an alsatian. A pot one. It flew out of a window in — that street.'

'Oh, that's it, eh? Aha, that's a good one. Couldn't quite place the alsatian could we, Mrs Vye?'

'It probably didn't hit me anyway. It was just in the . . .' I was going to say 'in the gutter beside me', but I suddenly couldn't be bothered.

'Ah. Aha? Well — let's not think about these things, eh? Everything's all right now. Boy-friend all right too, I hear. Nothing to make a fuss about.'

The two children on the doorstep had had fine white hair and dirty noses. One child was leaning over the other child. They had thin arms and were playing a game with chalk on the pavement. You could tell they spent a lot of time together. I looked at the doctor and he had on his hurrying-on look. You could tell that he knew the signs when he might be told something he didn't want to know.

'Tell you what,' he said, looking at his watch. 'Let's make it Monday. Next Monday back to school, eh? Stupid day to start really, Friday, anyway. Give her till Monday shall we, Mrs Vye? Never do anything the first day anyway or never did when I went to school. Let's say Monday,' (How he went on!) 'and just you keep away from any more alsatians.'

I heard him still on about Monday as he went downstairs

and mother being bright in her housemaster's wife voice, not saying half she really wanted to.

Now it is an odd thing, but when I really want to do something badly I often do everything I can possibly think of instead. It's not at all like the way some ghastly people have of 'leaving the best till last' and that sort of thing – eating all round the jam tart, drooling over how nice it's going to be when there's only the jam left. I've never understood this, and in fact if I was given the chance I would eat the jam and leave the pastry every time.

I don't know what it is. If I have a nice bit of homework or a good story to write, or if I get an idea for a poem, I just start doing anything – cleaning out my dressing-table drawer or scrubbing the draining board or going round to Florence's to talk about whether we can go to the pictures on Saturday. Once I had a marvellous idea for this opera we're going to have when I was in the front room with a bag of dried peas – I can't remember why I had the dried peas in there – and I spilled them all over the floor with excitement or something; and rather than going and getting a dust-pan and brush, I decided to pick up EVERY SINGLE ONE separately.

My father's the same. You should see him preparing to write his articles. He tidies his desk, brushes the fireside, winds the clock, shakes the clock, opens the back of the clock and takes all its insides out. Then he throws all the bits away. Then he gathers them all up again and stands looking at them for half an hour. Then he arranges them in rows, scratches his head, picks his teeth, sits down and takes his shoes off and smells them. Then he puts his head in his hands for an hour or two and then he shouts, 'Oh shut up all of you out there,' and starts typing. When we tell him about it he is surly. 'It's nervous,' he says, 'I'm only thinking.'

I'm a bit the same.

Another thing about me is that I often have to make great preparations for the next step after the actual nice thing is done, and I think this is part of the same peculiarity. Animals do it too – dogs go to sleep in exactly the right way, in a very particular way after they've eaten their dinners, for example. I realized that I was being just like some sort of an animal when I got up after my tremendous sleep after the air-raid. On the Sunday evening I became brisk as a bee.

I polished my shoes and even my schoolbag, I sharpened my pencils, marked my rubber, cleaned out my gas mask and arranged everything on the sewing-machine in the kitchen ready, even gloves and pixie hood. I laid out my gym-slip and clean blouse and other clothes and gave my clean stockings, vest and knickers a good shake.

'Aren't you overdoing it?' Florence asked. She'd been round for supper. 'It's only school. It's same as ever.'

I said I'd got everything in a mess and was having a clean-up and I began slamming dust out of the books and stacking up the satchel, putting the blue exercise book in the back.

'Did you do anything?'

'What?'

'Work'

'No. Did you?'

'I read a bit of *Romeo and Juliet*.'

'Did we have to?'

'If we felt like it.'

'Oh well, I'll just say I didn't.'

'I'm going now. Will you set me?'

'No, I'm going to bed early. I'm getting the early train.'

'You're barmy,' she said.

And in the morning, neat and tidy, I got out at Cleveland Spa Station at five minutes to eight and set off for Miss Philemon's flat. It was still dark, or just lightening over the sea. I stood against the wooden railings on the edge of the esplanade and looked across the bay at the fat cliffs, where on the top there was a barrage balloon on a string coming out of a lorry. Not beautiful at all. 'I'd better go over,' I thought and turned to cross the road. Then I decided all at once not to bother and I went to school instead and waited on the shoe-bags' steps until the train-line arrived at eight-thirty.

I didn't put the notebook in my desk but kept it in my satchel.

On the Tuesday and the Wednesday I caught the ordinary train and didn't go near the esplanade. On Wednesday afternoon, in French, I thought I heard Miss P.'s feet flipping about outside on her short cut and I nearly asked to be excused so that I could take her the book. But then again, I decided not to.

On the Thursday old Dobbs asked for any more poems. It was the last day today, she said. They had to be posted tomorrow. Quite a lot of people had one, even Florence who hadn't said a word about going in for the competition, and Dobbs made some jolly jokes about last-minute inspiration which nobody thought very funny. 'Not you then, Jessie-Carr?' she asked all bright and breezy and I said 'No, Miss Dobbs.'

The next morning, Friday, I persuaded Florence to get the early train and I said 'Let's go along the prom., it's only half a minute more. It's not like going down The Cut or anything,' and she said all right. When we got outside Miss P.'s, on the other side of the road we started horsing about and I hung upside down by my feet and hands on the railing, like a carcase on a pole and Florence said 'What are you, venison?' and I laughed terribly loudly. Florence said, 'Aren't you rather old for that sort of thing?' and I said, 'It's the railings that are rather old. I'm going to fall into the sea and drown,' and I did an imitation of someone drowning, until a window opened across the road and Miss P.'s head came out. 'Shoo,' she called, 'shoo. You girls – are you ours? I can't see. Whoever you are get off those railings, they're not safe,' and we got off and ran away as if we'd been Rowley or absolute babies.

When I got to school I found I'd left my satchel on the railings and I ran back for it and swung it to and fro wondering whether to go across. But I didn't again.

After dinner, when we set off back to school, I said I had a pain and felt sick and bent over my arms and held my stomach. 'I must dash,' I said, and ran over the road, up the grand steps to the School in the direction of the W.C.'s, and the others went on. When I got to the cloister where I'd been before I asked someone where the Staff Room was and when I found it I banged on the door. A mistress I didn't know answered it smoking a cigarette and with a newspaper in her hand bent back at the crossword. 'Miss Philemon goes home to lunch,' she said. 'She's not in school now.'

'But you might catch her at the side gates,' she called. 'She sometimes walks back through the sea-wood.'

17

I climbed the wide steps at the side of the school and hung about. The empty dinner-cans were stacked about the gates like milk churns: four big containers, labelled 'stew', two 'veg' and one 'sweet'. I wondered if they'd been cleaned out inside or if they were sent back with bits in and I turned away quickly and stood just outside on the pavement. The road leading to the sea-wood was empty.

I leaned on the gate post and saw the door of the Headmistress's house open and Miss LeBouche come out shutting the door neatly behind her. She looked both ways before she crossed the empty road. She had a sort of smile on her face. A gust of wind blew suddenly and flapped a bundle of papers in her arms. She protected them and walked with great control. Because of this gift I have I knew what she was thinking: she was thinking about Iris Ingledew's scholarship to Cambridge which we'd all heard about at prayers – even down in the Juniors. Iris Ingledew was going to make the school famous one day Miss Macmillan had said and you could see Miss LeBouche was feeling very delighted. She turned the corner and went off towards the main gates and didn't see me.

Inside the school a bell rang – a buzzer thing, loud and long, and a few girls who had been knocking a hockey ball about the field behind me stopped and began to move indoors. One of them threw her stick up in the air and shrieked and another pushed her in the small of the back. 'I'm perished,' she shouted and a gust of wind swirled round the field and blew gravel in my eyes and I turned my face into the gate-post.

What on earth was I doing there, I wondered. Miss Philemon wasn't coming. She didn't teach every day – only the brilliant ones who were just leaving. She was too old to do any more. Anyway, why was I wanting to see her? The poems were all in. Iris Ingledew would win the school prize anyway – probably the prize the whole country was going in for, too. There could hardly be anyone cleverer. Miss P. wouldn't be interested in mine, even if she came. And she wasn't coming.

Another bell went and my stomach lurched. The second bell – I'd have to go. I lifted my head and I saw Miss Philemon coming unhurriedly along the road in deep conversation with Iris Ingledew.

When they got to me, Iris laughed and said, 'Well, goodbye,' and went running past me down the steps putting a finger on my head in a kindly sort of way as she went by. She looks like that girl on the Ovaltine advertisements, Iris, all rosy and golden-haired with healthy-looking eyes. She ought to have sheaves of corn under each arm. You'd never think she was clever.

She ran off across the cloister and Miss P. stood still and looked at me but didn't seem to be seeing me. 'Well I never!' she said, and began to beam and beam. 'Well I never. How splendid! Well I never!' 'Please Miss Philemon . . .' 'Well, I *am* delighted. Well I never!'

I thought, 'I suppose she's just heard about the scholarship. But that's funny, she'd have known before this. We all were told this morning and old Miss P. would have known first. What can it be?'

'Well I never!' said Miss P., chuckling and set off down the steps.

'Miss *Philemon*!'

She turned. 'Oh Jessica, I didn't see you. What is it, dear?'

'I want to ask you something.'

'To ask me something?'

'I've got to. It's urgent. It's very urgent.'

'Yes of course. Shall we sit down? Ought you to be here?'

'No. I'm going to be late. I'll be in a mess. But I've got to ask you something.'

'Let's sit down. What a wind! Dear me, the dust.' She sat on one of the tins labelled stew.

'Could we – could we perhaps sit somewhere else?' I asked. 'I think it might still perhaps have got some in it.'

'Indeed yes.' She shot off again. 'They found a dish-cloth in one of them one day you know. But perhaps you'd better not say.'

We sat on a seat across the road in a bus shelter with the glass knocked out of it, in the teeth of the wind.

'Well now?'

'Well – it's just – it's very urgent because it's the last day.'

'The Last Day?'

'For sending in poems. For the competition. But actually it's not only that.'

'Tell me.'

'Well, can you tell me please whether it is true that if you are really pleased with something you've done you ought to destroy it?'

'A poem?'

'Yes.'

Miss Philemon covered her face with her fingers for a while and the wind howled round her feet and swirled more gravel about. 'This is Miss Dobbs?' she asked.

'Yes. She said if you don't, later on you'll be ashamed.'

'Ashamed,' she said, 'ashamed. Yes. Now. Let us take this sentence to pieces. First, what do you mean by "really pleased"? This is the core, "really pleased". You have written a poem with which you are "really pleased"?'

'Not exactly, but it seems – all right.'

'Ah?'

'Well, I can't change it.'

'Yes?'

'It is – it's complete. All in one. It's all right.'

'Do you feel, "See what *I* have done?" Do you *swell*?'

'No,' I said. 'It's just all right. I keep going back to it and it's all right. I've never done that before.'

'You're not telling all the truth.'

I folded my arms under my armpits and shook with the cold and said, 'No.' She said, 'Try again.'

'I think it's wonderful,' I said. 'It's perfect. It's new. It's like a present. It is quite complete.'

'You are proud of it?'

'I'm sort of dazed. I'm worried because it came in a sort of dream. I just got out of bed – I was in a funny mood. It was after the raid. After Dunedin Street. I was in Dunedin Street in Shields East the day you were on the bus at the end of the holidays and I got in. There'd been a raid. I'd been in it.'

'I wondered,' she said, 'you *were* dirty, Jessica!'

'And I got home and ages after – ages after, the next day, I was terribly sort of queer and I wrote this poem. It came complete – it wasn't about the raid. Actually it's about that maniac – I didn't have to alter anything.'

'I think,' she said after a long time, 'I think that it is very unlikely that this poem is any good. It sounds like a poem written out of a dream. This is quite common. A number of poets have composed poetry in their dreams. But when they have written it down – and it must be done at once as you open your eyes and even then you never seem to get beyond the first few lines – it seldom amounts to anything much. Coleridge, of course, once composed a miraculous poem in his sleep. We only have a little of it. He had two or three hundred lines ready to write down, but the doorbell rang and there was someone on business to see him, and when he'd gone Coleridge found that the rest of the poem had gone too. It had faded away. He never remembered it . . .'

'So it can be?'

'With provisions.'

'Provisions?' (I didn't know what she meant – I thought of sandwiches and corn beef and things.)

'Provisions. Things to be taken into account. Kubla Khan – Coleridge's poem – was good because Coleridge wrote it, not because it came out of a dream. Do you see? It had to be his dream, not anyone's dream. It was a particular kind of dream because he had been taking opium – he took it for his aches and pains and it was his destroyer, his devil – but not anyone who took opium could have dreamed his dream. On his lap was a book he had been reading as he fell asleep and about ten of the words in the poem are in the book, and lots of people had read the book: but none of them could have written Kubla Khan. On the whole I think poems don't crawl out of dreams. They are knocked out of rocks.

'Children write poetry without pain or dreams of course,' she said. 'Sometimes poem after poem pours out – lovely poems. Before you're say ten, that is. You will remember.'

I said yes, but this wasn't like that.

She said, 'No. But you're not happy about it Jessica?'

'No,' I said, realizing I wasn't, 'no!'

'Yet you think it's perfect? Wonderful? A present?'

'Yes. No. Oh Miss Philemon, I don't want to talk about it. I don't want to read it again. I'm going.'

'Have you got it there?'

'Yes,' and I got the exercise book. 'It's on the back page.'

'Well, let me read it. Leave it to me. I'll certainly not put it in for the competition if I think it would be painful. Miss

Dobbs is quite right. One could die with shame for some of the things one was proud of once.'

I said thank you and she lifted up one of her midget hands and said, 'Wait.'

There was a long pause and she said, 'No. I've changed my mind, I don't think I care whether you are ashamed. Miss Dobbs and I differ on this point. I think I am assuming ... I think I am UNDERESTIMATING you. Poets on the whole are not much given to shame. Poets on the whole don't slink. They burn and suffer and get torn to bits – and they drink and grow fat and quarrel and die. They cut themselves to pieces and destroy their relations. They are bitter and mad and sad and heavy of heart. It's not a soft way, Jessica; but at least they're not ashamed.'

She stood up then and pulled her poor battered hat well down on her head and said, 'This poem is probably no good. Something dictated it. It may have been something thin and weak or proud and self-satisfied. On the other hand it *may* be good and yet in three months' time you won't think anything of it at all. You will have thrown it off. You won't want to talk about it. You will have moved on to something else, or some other experience, some other puzzle to solve. Poets don't feel ashamed of their poems, but they do often just forget them. They let them go. They let them blow about like leaves. That's what Browning meant when he said only God knows what it means now.'

I think I said before – in the conversation between Ma and Mrs F-S which I heard through the floor – that I have a terribly good memory, and so I really do remember all this, every word: though I must say I didn't altogether understand it.

She picked up her case and said, 'I will telephone Miss Macmillan to say that you will be late, and I promise you that if it is a good poem I will post it. Now off you go, and please dear, *think*, and go back the right way this time. Keep away from the sea-wood today.' And off she went, over the road, down the steps and into the school. She was wagging her head and still talking, her hair in wisps under her awful hat, her little hands like claws on her case handle, most terribly late for her lesson.

18

The school was bombed that night. A land-mine fell in the middle of the quadrangle just at supper time and blew the whole place to bits.

Not only the school, either. Another one fell on the Headmistress's house and put an end to the shilling dinners for ever and destroyed the pillar box at the gate where the poetry competition entries had been posted to catch the seven-fifteen, and none of them was ever seen again. Miss Birdwood and Miss LeBouche were seen again because they had set off just beforehand to a first-aid class in the town hall, Miss LeBouche posting the entries on the way.

Three other bombs fell on Cleveland Spa, and we heard them all falling right over in Cleveland Sands. My father ran into the house to see that we were all right – he was on A.R.P. duty – and he said, 'Cleveland Spa seems to be getting it tonight. What on earth do they want with Cleveland Spa?' It turned out later that it was an English plane trying to land that had dropped the bombs. It was damaged and was going to crash and thought it would get rid of them in the sea first. However they fell a bit too late and all over the place and there was no school in the morning.

We all set out as usual on Monday of course to see what we should do – my father came with me as a matter of fact – and Miss Macmillan was at the station looking very severe and pale and said, 'Seniors only. The Juniors are to go home. You will all hear about Future Plans as soon as possible;' and going home in the train we were all terribly noisy and carried on like anything about how lovely having no school. My father didn't say a thing, just sat there in the carriage looking out of the window. Cissie Comberbach was there – going home with Dottie where she'd been for the weekend and because there were so few buses to her aunt's farm from school, and my father leaned over to her and said, 'I haven't met you have I?' and she said, 'No, and I'm not stopping neither. I'm from London and I'm goin' 'ome.'

We never saw her again after that. My father said, 'Why didn't you have that funny little thing home ever?' and I said, 'Cissie *Comberbach*!' and he said, 'She looked utterly wretched.' I was very surprised indeed because he is usually right about people when he notices them. I wondered why it was that this gift I have of knowing what people are thinking hadn't worked with Cissie. Then I began to wonder if it was a gift at all and if I haven't imagined the whole thing. Then I began to think about how unpopular I am, and I got very depressed indeed.

Well, as many of the Seniors as possible were moved into the Junior School and the rest of us were divided up round the neighbourhood in the Board Schools (Florence called them the

Bored Schools, oh ha and ha) and the private schools, such as they were, until they could get ours put up again. They started with the private schools, and dished us out down the alphabet so that Florence B. went to a place called The Gables where they learned needlework and which spoon to use at dinner parties. Helen Bell went there, too, and down to Dottie H. But by the time they'd got to the Vs, they were pushing us any-where and I had to go to St Wilfred's at the end of our road, across the road from the church and my father doing the Scripture – which he knows much less of than Miss Dobbs.

I loved this school though. They never noticed what you were doing there were so many in the class. You could just sit and read a book and enjoy yourself all day; and I loved the way they talked and began to talk like it, too, and Ma began to go really mad and say whatever father wrote in *The New Statesman* about everyone being equal, her family had always spoken the King's English, and father said it all depended which king you meant.

And now I will speed the story up, and describe only the two main episodes of this time. Both are depressing and could be skipped if you are pressed. Probably I would skip them myself if it were not for old Dobbs saying you have to cut out everything that isn't absolutely necessary. It seems to me that when you get started doing this you end up with noth-ing left at all; and I don't at all care for having nothing left at all. It is very alarming, like the dreams you get about people walking through you in the street not noticing you are there.

Well, the first episode was when Florence and I were in

our front room one Sunday afternoon. She still came round at weekends and sometimes brought her so-called homework with her. This Sunday she had just said something I didn't think much of and I had replied, 'Away!'

'"Away",' she said. 'Whatever does that mean?' I told her. (They say it at St Wilfred's all the time and it means come here, go there, hello, goodbye, it's a grand day, it's a nasty day, how's your father? – everything.) 'How gharsley,' she said.

I said, 'You're like the Fanshawes.'

'Who're they?'

'The people I told you about. At Christmas. I wrote you a letter about them. Didn't you get it?'

'I may of.'

'"May of" – that doesn't sound like The Gables.'

She said, 'What are you reading?'

'Something a girl gave me. Listen, "The pains seized her in their iron claws. She gasped, 'Adrian! Adrian! Save me! I'd no idea it was like this.'" She's having a baby.'

'I hope you're enjoying it.'

'Marvellous! It's about a man called Mr Hope-Merton. Mrs Hope-Merton is having a baby. A lovely little baybee.'

'How spiflicating for her.'

'I say you *are* getting like the Fanshawes!'

'Who're the Fanshawes?'

That's how we went on.

After a bit she said she'd finished *Romeo and Juliet* and was reading *Hamlet*, which for some reason made me wild and I began to read her some more bits about the Hope-Mertons.

'For crying out loud!' she said, 'I don't want to hear about it. You're like Cissie was about her aunt's cows.'

'I suppose they never mention such things at The Gables.'

'Oh yes they do. They never talk about anything else – all babies and boyfriends and how they're not feeling so well today.'

I said it was the same at St Wilfred's – all babies and boys and trash. In *front* of the boys, too.

'Do you talk to the boys?'

'No. They shout at each other all the time. Through half the lessons too. Miss Nattress comes round with a ruler. Great big boys.'

'What! She *hits* them?'

'She says, "That will do, Jackson. Hold out your hand."'

'And he does?'

'Well Jackson's actually a girl.'

'She hits the girls?'

'Yes – not me because of father. We all get called by our surnames.'

'So you're called Vye? How *gharsley*.'

I said, away, they liked being smacked. I told her I liked it there and that I liked them and that 'away' was a Saxon survival, father said. 'You're a snob,' she said, but didn't mean it. It was a very friendly conversation.

We lay around the front room very quiet for a bit, except for a few bursts of machine-gun fire from Rowley who had got a gun-emplacement behind the sofa with two of the six-foot candlesticks poking out. F. was deep in *Hamlet*, or pretending. She kept on at intervals asking why I wasn't reading anything but this Hope-Merton book and I said I didn't know.

She threw down *Hamlet* and looked out of the window. 'I say,' she said, 'look at those two queer boys at the bus stop. They haven't any trousers on. They'll catch their deffs,' and I looked and saw Giles and Christian muffled up round their necks in rolls of striped scarves which narrowed down to short coats and bare red legs and ankle socks.

I said, 'It's Christian.'

'Who is he?'

'I told you about him. I think it's their school uniform.'

'Good heavens! Even for that size!'

'I think so. They're at some school in the mountains some-where. They believe in funny things there. They're terribly healthy. I suppose it's Half Term.' (It was nearly March now.)

'Which one's Christian? The fair one?'

'Yes.'

'Hey,' she said, 'isn't that the boy Cissie saw you with at the station? She said he was marvellous. She said he was like Leslie Howard.'

'Yes,' I said, and realized it wasn't true any more. Christian's hair was clipped all over his head like a tooth-brush, upright and brisk. He was wearing glasses and his long legs looked rather bent, with oval blue knees. His face was very thin and doleful.

'I like the look of the other one better,' she said. 'He seems to have a bit of life about him.'

Giles was also doleful, but every now and then he gave Christian a great nudge with the side of his body. Once he knocked him into the gutter. He was talking very vigorously. Christian, hands in his pockets, eyes down, just stood there, looking at the weeds growing out of the soil round the bottom of the bus stop.

'What they doing I wonder?'

'You'd better go and see.'

'Why? They can come over.'

'They don't seem to know what they think they're doing. Good heavens!'

Christian suddenly took a fist out of his pocket and swung it at Giles like a mallet. Giles tottered and began to slam back. 'You'd better go,' said Florence, 'or there'll be a murder.'

'I wanna come, I wanna come. Liff me! Liff me!'

'You stay there, Rowley.'

'I wanna come.' He scrambled over the sofa and clung on to me.

'Oh, all right then. You'll freeze without a coat and I'm not stopping to get you one and I don't care.' And I dragged him over the road under my arm and thumped him down on the pavement and said, 'Hello, Christian.'

They stopped fighting.

'Oh hum. Hello,' said Giles. Christian scowled. 'We were just coming to see you,' said Giles.

'My name's Rowley,' said Rowley. 'Please can I play balancing?'

'Where?' said Giles.

'On the alockments.'

Giles lifted him on to the fence of the allotments that run along the other side of our road. 'Steady now,' he said. 'Hold on to my finger.' And Rowley cried, 'Yoo hoo! Look at me, I'm grand as a king.'

Giles said, peering through his glasses, 'You'll catch cold without a coat on,' and unwound his scarf and draped it round him. The two of them walked away from the bus stop with their heads level, holding finger-tips like a minuet. Giles is a kind boy.

I was left alone with Christian. He had a scar on his forehead which might be why he'd had his hair cut off. It was quite a big scar and purplish in colour. I got hold of the bus stop and began to swing on it and he began to kick the pavement.

In the end I asked him if he'd seen the people again.

'What people?' he said.

'The ones who took us in.'

'Took us in?'

'Yes – the ones your mother said your father was going to give a present to.'

He said, 'Present? I don't know what you're talking about.'

'Those people. The man in the corner and the woman with no legs.'

'I never saw those people.'

'You did. Ern – there was Ern. He got you some tea.' But he just looked at me as if I was mad. 'You're making it Up.'

'I'm not. Are you crazy? Don't you remember? The man

who came from Peterborough. He said about the zip fastener.'

'I don't remember.' He honestly seemed not to remember.

'Don't you remember anything? You did just after. Your mother said.'

He turned away and said, 'Were you all right getting back?'

'Oh yes, fine. A bus came in after a bit.'

He stood gazing at the horrible thick stump's of the brussels sprouts on the allotments and I said, 'It's quite all right you know. You didn't cause it.'

'What d'you mean?' He curled his top lip like a villain.

'You didn't drop that bomb.'

'What're you talking about?'

'You didn't cause it. All you did was put your hands in the air.'

'Oh for God's sake!'

'You just said, putting your hands in the air, that you wanted it destroyed.'

'Oh, shut up.' He was kicking the post now. 'You don't think I imagine *I* did it! Good heavens!'

'That plane had been loaded up ages before, miles away, in Brest or Dusseldorf or somewhere. He was off course. Everyone said he was off course. It was a random. Everybody said that bomb was a random. He wouldn't just send one bomb, one aeroplane to the docks on a Sunday afternoon.'

He muttered.

'What?' I demanded, very firm. 'What d'you say?'

'I just said it was a bit odd – just one aeroplane, just there.'

'Well, it was fantastic. But it would be a lot more fantastic if you believed you'd put it there – created it – the man and the aeroplane and the bomb. You don't really think you can create metal and bones and brains and things, do you? You don't think you can tell God what to do?'

'I don't believe in God. I'm not talking about God.'

'Yes you are. You are thinking you are God.'

'Look, why don't you shut up?'

'D'you think all those people you and father were talking about – would think things like this? This Marx and Bernard Shaw lot? Do you think they believed they could make aeroplanes appear out of the air and kill people? What d'you think you are? Ali Baba or someone?'

He began to smile a bit.

'My goodness!' I said. 'My goodness, and you told me to grow up! You told me I didn't know how to think! Come on, Rowley,' (they were minueting back) 'we've got to go in. You're blue.'

'It was all pretty queer,' he said. 'You do hear of funny things. Some very fine thinkers have been interested in spiritualism.'

'For crying out loud!' I cried out loud, 'have you never attempted to use your head? You can't look at things straight, Christian Fanshawe-Smithe. You don't examine the facts. You don't use your head.' It was like father speaking. It was terrific and he was actually blushing. But at the same time l knew that I'd never have the feeling I had about him, when I first saw him looking into the fire – not ever again.

19

The second thing in this empty time was *Jude the Obscure.*

I've said at the beginning that I'm not able to tell lies for one reason and another, but I suppose I did come pretty near it when Florence asked me why I didn't read anything any more and I said I didn't know. What I should have said was, 'I do.' I should have said, 'I read all the time. In fact, I never did read before. Little did you know,' I should have said, 'how I read.' I am even a bit afraid of the way I read. It's like mother was when Rowley was coming, eating all the crusts off the bread. She just couldn't stop eating bread. She'd see a loaf on the table and start cutting all its sides off, then turn it over and carve its bottom off. Then she'd say 'It's really dreadful the way I'm eating bread,' and her arm would come reluctantly out and she'd start carving little bits off the slopes, until the bread stood all naked and white. And after a while she'd say, 'Oh dear, I'd love another crust.'

I started reading like this the very next day after the school was bombed. I went down to the Public Library and stayed there all day, except at dinner time. I went the next day and the next, and the next week when they'd fixed up which school I was to go to, I went straight from school until seven when it closed. Ma gave me a sandwich to take with me, and the library is only down the road and Mrs Baxter's on the desk stamping the books, so she didn't worry. I heard her through the floor saying to father, 'She'll read her eyes out,' but he said, 'It's the best thing when there's a death. Leave her alone.'

The library was opened just before the war and it's still a bit new-looking and not terribly over-used. The children's department I got through years ago, and although we're not supposed to use the rest of it till we're fourteen, Mrs Baxter doesn't seem to mind as long as we're quiet, so I wander round all over. Most of the books are terrible looking love-stories, all tattered by the old ladies who take them out every Saturday, but there are a few good ones that have got in by accident, and it all smells nice, and there are seats put here and there at the ends of the rows to sit and look the books over, though if an old lady comes along you're expected to get up, which is a nuisance.

The best part of the library is the Reference Room, which is at the back and very small and friendly. The Library is the first floor of what used to be a grand house some old millionaire from the ironworks built, and the Reference Room was his study. You can tell from the feel of it that he didn't do much studying – it's got a lovely heavy drowsy feeling. He must have gone in there to put his hankie over his head after dinner. There's a lovely fireplace in there made of stone with scrolls down the side, and they've left a beautiful gold bell-handle like a serpent at the side of it, so that when the fire went down you could ring for one of the slaves to bring the coal, and another pipe or port or something. Sometimes they light a fire in the grate even now, just to stop the pipes icing up I suppose, and in front of it the reference desk stands – there's only one – with a very low reading lamp on it with a dark green shade that makes one ring on the desk and leaves the rest of the room in darkness.

I went in the reading room every single afternoon after school from four o'clock till seven, and there was absolutely never anybody else there but me.

Well, at first I just read and read a marvellous book of cartoons by Heath Robinson, of things all tied together with string. They were terribly funny and for some reason they made me feel comfortable. When I got to the end of this book, I turned back to the beginning and started again. Then after about four days I thought I'd look for something else and saw there was a bookcase on the wall beside me labelled 'English Classics'. (Actually that's all there was in the whole reference room except for an Encyclopaedia and the Heath Robinson book.) There were several hundred books – novels – in this case, and I decided all of a sudden that I would read them all. I felt that since I was a writer beyond all possible doubt, I ought at some time to go through the works of other writers, and that I probably would never have such a good chance again. I am a very quick reader – I have as I've said, very large, squarish eyes that seem to be able to fit over a good patch of the page. My mother says, 'You can't be taking it in,' but I do. I wish I read slower as a matter of fact because I can't get books to last. They said the school wouldn't be repaired till after the Easter holidays so I thought I had every chance of reading everything in the case by then, and I decided to start alphabetically. Each night I took the book I was reading as the buzzer went at seven o'clock, home under my coat and read it till I went to sleep and took it to school next morning and read it there through lessons for most of the day (I sat at the back) and in this way had read most of Jane Austen in three weeks, even though there are certain things I very much dislike in her books. I won't go into them now.

I don't know if you've noticed but if you want to become one of the English Classics it's a good idea to be up in the top half of the alphabet. There are a tremendous lot of As and Bs and Ds and – down to about H. Then there's hardly anything at all, until you get to all the Richardson, Scott, Thackeray lot. It's rather depressing really and you don't feel you're making much progress when after a month you're just past the Brontës – and when you see how many Dickens's are coming. But I must say I loved the first two or three weeks.

Then I decided I'd skip about a bit and read one of the Es – a very strange looking man called George Eliot, with ringlets and watery eyes. It was called *Silas Marner* and it was marvellous. And then I decided to read an H and chose *Jude the Obscure* by Thomas Hardy.

I hope I never read another book so utterly terrible as this. It is a marvellous book, and I didn't skip any of it, and

I read on and on and on; but all the time I was thinking of Thomas Hardy, of the terrible sorrows and sadness of him. It seemed terrible to me that anyone who knew that he was a writer beyond all possible doubt should have not one glimmer, not one faintest trace of happiness in him. There was one thing that he said that beat in my head, over and over and over again. It was at the point where poor Jude just misses meeting someone who might have changed the whole terrible pattern of his life. If he had, who knows, says Hardy, then all might yet have been well. Then he adds, but this did not happen, this good fortune, BECAUSE IT NEVER DOES.

I could not get this terrible idea out of my mind, even while I read on to see what happened next, taking it all in and understanding it – but only on the top. Underneath there was this awful, awful idea: BECAUSE IT NEVER DOES.

I had just reached the part when Jude's eldest son had hanged both his little brothers and hitched them up on the back of the bedroom door like dressing gowns when a hand came down on to the book from out of the shadows beyond the reading lamp, and it was Mrs Baxter. 'Jessica!' she said, 'I'd no idea you were still here. The buzzer went ten minutes ago. Whatever are you reading? It must be very exciting.' She picked *Jude* up and held it near her spectacles for a moment, twisting the lamp upwards so that she could see. She gave the most frightful sort of yelp after a minute and nearly dropped it. 'Jess, *dear*!' she cried, 'wherever on earth! What is this terrible book?' I said it was an English Classic. 'It must be removed from the library,' she said. 'It's a most horrible book. What would your father say? Oh, Jessica, you mustn't read such a horrible book!'

I said it was by Thomas Hardy.

'I don't care if it is by William Shakespeare, you are NOT to read it. I will speak to the Librarian to have it taken off the shelves.' And I think she must have done, because it's certainly not there now.

'Now come with me,' she said. 'Come along dear,' and she led me off into the main library to a shelf full of velvety-looking, thin sort of books, and picked one out. 'You take this home,' she said, 'much more the thing. No – don't worry, I'll mark it out on my ticket.' She seemed in a great state about it all. 'Off you go, dear. Now have a nice read of that one in bed. We can't have you reading Thomas Hardy – we'll have you getting all depressed. Your father will never forgive me.'

I went off home with her book under my arm, and in through the front door and into the kitchen where there was some supper in the oven not too dry.

BECAUSE IT NEVER DOES, I kept saying. BECAUSE IT NEVER DOES.

I heard a murmuring noise from the front room and Ma called me in to do the polite to some people who'd called – the Jamiesons. They used to teach at the school when father was a schoolmaster and they'd gone to live in Greece or somewhere. They'd just escaped from it as a matter of fact, with 'only the clothes they stood up in', I'd heard mother say.

BECAUSE IT NEVER DOES.

'How do you do, Mrs Jamieson. How do you do, Mr Jamieson.' They looked pretty good clothes to me. She was in a better dress than mother. '*Jess!*' she said, all sorrowful, holding on to my hand, 'Little Jess!' (I've noticed as a matter of fact that when people are in a public sort of mess – like after their husbands or wives have died and you're all being sorry for them, they look at YOU as if you're the one to be sorry for.) 'So this is little *Jess!*' *I* felt like saying, 'Oh I'm all right. You don't have to worry about me. Everything's fine here.'

And then I heard it again, that awful, awful cry. IT NEVER DOES, IT NEVER DOES.

Father came whirling in – he hadn't seen them yet – 'Jim!' he cried, 'Ellen!' and hugged them. They started to talk like mad about Crete. '. . . never have tried to defend it . . . No one with any foresight . . .' I couldn't see why they were surprised. Why did they expect anything good? Everything came to nothing in the end.

I had Mrs Baxter's book on the floor by my feet – I was sitting forward on a low arm-chair and I began to flick the pages over, quietly so they wouldn't notice. It was a book called *Lingering in Lakeland*, and seemed to be full of sentences about 'the pastel twilight', 'stopping for a minute to hear the clear and lonely call of the curlew', and so on. I read on and slowly I realised I was reading the most awful, dreadful, ghastly book I had ever read in my life, worse even than Mrs Hope-Merton, worse than *The Cloister and the Hearth*. I looked at a photograph of the author in the front, standing sideways on a moor, with a dog beside him and a pipe stuck out of the side of an awful, honest sort of face and gazing at the sunset. There was something about his silhouette that reminded me of someone.

'Still — we mustn't lose heart,' said Mrs Jamieson brightly, as I turned the book over to see who'd written it.

It was by Arnold Hanger.

20

I don't know how I got through the time between that evening and the time when school reopened. I still went to the library every day and read all through every lesson at St Wilfred's, but I wasn't able to lose myself any more. I went back to the Ds and started Dickens – I'd skipped him because I thought I was going to enjoy him, in this queer way I spoke about of putting things off that I'm going to enjoy: but I somehow couldn't enjoy him at all. I knew, when I started *David Copperfield* – 'Whether I shall turn out to be the hero of my own life . . .' etc., that if I'd only read it before it would have been the best thing that I'd ever found. But somehow something had gone. I just wished that I had never, never gone to that lecture at my kindergarten school, or that I had been sent out for laughing before Arnold H. started talking. I wished with all my heart that nobody had ever put it into my head that I was a writer.

Because it wasn't so. Obviously it wasn't so. If he thought the pastel sunset was good and the lonely cry of the curlew and also thought I was good, then it meant that

I was like the pastel sunset and the lonely cry of the curlew. Miss Dobbs was right. I thought of the terrible poem I'd written and shown to Miss Philemon and I wanted to die. It was like finding out in those dreams you get, that standing in church in the middle of the Gloria you haven't got any clothes on.

I read on and on, Dickens after Dickens, not taking it in, turning the pages in the old iron-millionaire's study, wishing I'd never been born.

School opened up at the end of April – four weeks ago today. It was the most marvellous morning with great gusts of wind blowing the daffodils flat in the gardens as we walked up Norma Place to Big School for first-morning prayers. The sky was bright purple as if there was going to be a great storm of rain, and a few big drops did keep falling, and then great searchlights of sunshine would shine out. The sea was wild, flinging itself about in all directions, the waves rearing up, tearing in at angles to each other like a battlefield.

They were all talking like mad, and laughing. Miss Macmillan and Miss Pemberton who were taking the train-line looked happy, too. It was funny all being together again. Helen Bell was even smiling – (Her boyfriend seemed to have disappeared. Dottie said 'For goodness sake don't *mention* him.') She'd passed Grade VI piano while she'd been at The Gables, doing nothing else, and only thirteen! Florence had that crazy look on her face and kept saying mad, sober things. Miss Macmillan said it was nice to see her droll face again. Droll – that's exactly what Florence is.

Helen played the march for prayers and we all filed in and started with a minute's silence – 'and thanksgiving' said old LeBouche – and we were all pretty silent, though some of the little ones fooled about. Then LeBouche said 'God be in my head', and we all sat down and she said she must announce the new Head Girl, Bessy Lipton – a great, heavy, black-eyed girl with short legs. She stomped up to take the silver badge and back again with hardly a clap, because everybody was gasping and whispering to each other, 'Iris? Where's Iris?' and looking at the place where she had always stood beside the back radiator under the picture of a blindfold woman sitting on the world. But not only the picture and the radiator had gone. Iris had gone too.

'Iris Ingledew has left the school,' Miss LeBouche then gave out in a voice like dry leaves, 'in order to get married,' and the noise that went round then was like a spring tide. 'She has married a sergeant in the Tank Corps.

'But,' she went on, 'I have another and very delightful thing to announce which I am sure will make us all very proud indeed, and is a splendid start to our new life here today. I heard yesterday that a poem from this school – from among the hundreds of entries sent in from schools all over the country, from some of the finest schools in England, one of *our* entries is the winner. It will be printed in *The Times* tomorrow.'

'Iris Ingledew,' everyone still whispered.

'Bla and bla and bla,' she went on.

Florence pushed me. 'Go on,' she said.

'What?' I said.

'It's you, you fool.'

'Me? What for?'

'The poem.'

'The poem? *That* poem?'

'And now Jessica – Jessica Vye please. Will you come up and receive the cheque for twenty pounds.'

Everybody began to cheer and clap.

'Get *on*,' said Florence.

'What for?' I was all blank. She must have posted it in another pillar box on the way home.

'For the cheque.'

'What cheque?'

For the poem. GO UP AND GET THE FLIPPING CHEQUE.'

'But it was an awful poem,' I said. 'Good heavens, they're insane.'

Miss Dobbs leaned over, with her beard nearly in my face all sweet beams, and gently pushed me, 'Go along, dear. Up you go.'

I almost ran. 'Miss LeBouche,' I said, 'there's a mistake. It was a terrible poem. It was no good. They've made a mistake. It'll be someone else.'

She raised her voice, 'A cheque for twenty pounds,' she said, smiling all round and the cheering and clapping grew louder and louder. 'Sent in as a separate entry.' (Hurray! Hurray!)

'I can't take it. I'm sorry. It was a foul poem.'

'Take it.'

'No thanks. I don't want it.'

'Take it.' (Her glasses flashed.)

'I don't want it. It's a mistake. I'll look pretty silly

tomorrow when it's someone else's poem comes out. They've messed it up.'

'Nonsense. Take it.' She thrust the cheque into my hand and I went muttering back to my row, while they carried on like mad – all their round pink faces, cheering and shouting, all awed and excited and envious and smiling and Miss Dobbs quite purple in the neck. And they kept it up afterwards. All the staff kept coming up and saying, 'Jolly well done, Jessica', 'Can I see a copy now, Jessica?' 'We'll all be ordering *The Times* tomorrow, Jessica'. It was a very queer feeling. Even during the fourpenny dinner – people kept on, 'What you going to do with it, Jessica?'

Really to get away more than anything else I asked if I could go and buy the picture in the art shop, and they beamed and smiled and said, 'But *of course* you can', and when Florence and Helen and Dottie asked if they could come with me, they said, 'But *of course*.'

So after school, there we were just like last year going up Ginger Street towards Elsie Meeney's but stopping at the art shop which was on the opposite corner, all in the drizzly sea-fret that had taken over from the windy bright morning. Just like the day of the tea-party all over again – dismal.

The picture was still there in the window, and the shop was open, though it didn't look as though it would be and the woman in charge seemed rather uncertain about getting it out. 'It's very large,' she said. 'It's been there a very long time. And I think perhaps I ought to mention that it's – ahem – three pounds ten shillings. Do you children *have* such a great amount of money? I don't want to seem . . .'

I said, 'Hey – it's her!'

'What d'you say, dear?'

'We met you before.'

'Well now!' She stopped and peered at us and clasped her amber bangles together. 'Well now! Is that so!' She hadn't a clue.

I said, 'Please, I have quite enough money for the picture and I handed her the cheque and asked if she could give me the change. She peered at it. 'You have to pay this into a bank,' she said. 'I can't take it. '*The Times* newspaper.' My word! Are you a correspondent of that newspaper? My word!'

'Oh no! Please, I don't know any banks.'

'Well, suppose,' she said, 'I let you take this picture now and you give me an I.O.U.? Then when you've cashed the cheque you can just bring me back the notes. How will that be?'

'Oh well, yes,' I said. 'That's fine.'

'Now then just you hold the things as I get it out of the window. Dear me, the dust!'

I wrote on a piece of paper, 'I.O.U. Three pounds ten shillings, Jessica Vye,' and handed it over.

'Well now, I'll just get a cloth and clean it up a bit. Now just one minute.' And she disappeared and didn't come back. After five minutes Florence said, 'We'll miss the train.'

The others were getting restless too, and after a bit longer Dottie said, 'I'm off.'

'Oh wait a bit,' I said, 'it's her.'

'Her?' said Helen.

'Yes – you remember.'

'Remember what?'

'Well her, it's her. It's Mrs Loony Hopkins.'

'Whoever's she when she's at home?'

'Don't you remember?'

They didn't seem to. I couldn't believe it. After a minute they said, 'Come on we're going.' Florence stayed on a bit, picking things up and putting them down, but in the end she left, too, and I was all alone in the shop.

After ages I heard Mrs H. though and she came wandering in with a cloth in one hand and an orange in the other. 'Here,' she said, 'I looked everywhere. I knew I had it somewhere,' and she gave me the orange – I hadn't seen one since Christmas. 'Now,' she said, 'I can remember once in poor, poor Spain, going out into my garden and *picking* the oranges off the trees! I wonder if you will ever do that, child? Where are the other young girls?'

'They had to go. They didn't want to miss their train.'

'No indeed. Well you take it, dear, you take it. Here's the picture. Goodness how heavy! Goodbye, child, goodbye.'

I lugged the picture under one arm – it came nearly to my feet and it was very difficult and heavy. It had the most tremendous frame. In my other hand I had the orange and over my shoulder my school bag and gas-mask

Florence, I was glad to see, was still standing at the top of the subway. 'I waited,' she said. 'You'll never carry it alone.

What a frame – you'd think it was a Rembrandt or something.'

I said something about him being Rembrandt to all the world but he was Willie to me and asked her what Rembrandt's first name was. She just stared at me. She even looked a bit alarmed.

'You don't *honestly* not remember?' I said

'Who?'

'Well her – the woman in there.'

'In the art shop yes, she was that funny woman who came into Elsie Meeney's.'

'But don't you *remember* her?'

'Yes – of course I remember her. But I don't see what you're so excited about.

'The trouble with you, Jessica,' she said, 'is that you are all feelings. Why don't you use your head?'

'*What?*' I said.

'Why do you have to get so excited all the time? Don't get in such a *state* all the time. You exaggerate, that's your trouble. You see things out of focus, like cows.'

'Do cows?'

'Yes – they see things double the size.'

'Well, *The Times* newspaper didn't seem to mind.'

Of course I shouldn't have said it. I honestly don't know why I did say it. I suppose because usually Florence, though she pretends to be severe, is basically such an uncritical girl. I suddenly saw, I think, that she really rather loathes me sometimes.

'Walter de la Mare doesn't mind,' I said.

'Well I'd better go now,' she said and went off down the subway not looking back, leaving me with the picture on the pavement.

21

At first I turned back to the shop, thinking I'd take the picture back in and ask Mrs Loony H. to store it for me for a while; but I got a queer sensation looking through the glass. The place looked quite empty and dead as if no one had been in it for years. All the stuff inside – you could see if you put your face against the glass – looked dim, as though it were underwater. There was a chair with a round cane back and a shelf with a lot of china rabbits on it, blue and green and pink with fat ears – and a bead shawl draped over a screen, all in shadow. There was no sign we'd even disturbed the dust. It gave me the creeps a bit.

I pushed the picture over the road instead to the steps of Elsie Meeney's and somehow bumped it up them, first one, then the next. It looked exactly the same as at the tea-party – the same old doilies and empty shelves and curtains on a rail. I thought I saw Alice and the other one inside and I did just think, all of a sudden, of going in. It gave me a very pleasant feeling, actually, to think how I'd go in.

'It would give me great pleasure,' I would say, 'great pleasure, if you would accept this painting –'

'Oh we couldn't!'

'Yes, take it. It's just a small thing . . .'

'Oh Madam! It's beautiful! We couldn't.'

'Take it!'

But I couldn't really get at the door-handle when I thought about it, with the picture in the way. I could have leaned forward but there was the orange. I was thinking it out when I saw Alice come marching through the archway with a cigarette hanging out of her mouth and her sleeves rolled up. She had a very violent expression.

She saw me and her expression grew worse – you could see it was habit – and I bobbed down and let the picture fall slowly backwards against my head. I put the orange under my chin and spread my arms out and by getting up slowly I could balance it on my head, though what with my school-bag and my gas-mask I was shaky. It was glass-downwards and not very comfortable. I could see their two seedy old heads looking at me over the rail. 'It's that girl, Allus!' 'What girl?' 'That nasty argumentative girl that caused trouble.' Of course I couldn't *actually* see they were there because the orange kept my chin down.

I went very quietly down Ginger Street and nobody came by. As I've said before Cleveland Spa is the deadest town in the whole world – streets and streets of houses with heavy old curtains and neat front gardens and never a soul. In some streets there's about one old lady in every house. They were left over from the first war when all the men got killed and they've just had to sit ever since. I could only see the bottoms of their gates and gateposts today, and the lines on the pavements, but I knew exactly where I'd got to because of going up and down Ginger Street so often – six times a day counting the dinner hours; and even after not doing so all the time we were bombed I recognized every single inch. I wouldn't be surprised if when I'm old and they take me all doddering in a wheel-chair with my mouth hanging open and my chin nodding away, I'll know every inch still. It is surprising as a matter of fact how little of a thing you have to see to recognize it. Rowley for instance could tell a Ford car from a Rover car when he was still in his *pushchair*, and couldn't see more than wheels. It makes one very interested in eyes.

I didn't know where I'd decided to go, but after a while I found my feet were walking me on to the promenade. I passed the big stone gates that go down to the sea-wood, and went on steady and straight to the steps that led up to Miss Philemon's front door. The bottom step had always had a small piece missing from it as if someone had taken a bite. I paused and looking at the step, and gulping rather – it is difficult to hold an orange against your throat for long with a weight on your head – I seemed to see Miss Crake's old phiz looking down from above.

'Dora, there is something outside.'

'Is there, dear?'

'It's a picture. It is proceeding in this direction. There are legs beneath it.'

'How very extraordinary. Let me see. Just let me finish toasting this bread.'

'It is proceeding at about the height of an Upper Fourth.'

'Dash! I've dropped the butter down the bookcase.'

'It is proceeding at an awkward angle. It is turning in at the gate.'

'Why, I expect it's Jessica. Put on the kettle, dear.'

'Oh no – I'm wrong. It's turned back. It's going away. How strange.

When I got back to the sea-wood gates I had a flash of some sort of sense. I put the picture down and straightened up. 'You must look,' I said, and looked back at the windows where old C. and Miss P. ought to have been standing, Miss P. with the knife in one hand and the butter in the paper in the other, and their funny old faces asking questions. It was not as bad as I'd expected – just like any other bombed house.

I pushed the picture behind the little sentry-box thing where you used to have to buy a ticket to go to the sea-wood when there were men before the war to sell the tickets, and I went off down the steps and into the trees that grew all over the slope of curled-back leaves. The smell of the wild garlic was tremendous. It had begun to rain harder and you could hear the drops everywhere, but no wet came through. I went on and on down the narrow path, just plodding on, and it grew dark and miserable.

I came to the little side-path that led off, and I went down it. The wood had got much scruffier since last September. Some branches had come down through the winter and nobody had cleared them away. The wood had grown thicker and the trees seemed to stand closer together. After a while they thinned out and the bandstand came in sight

below in the rain. A lot of paint seemed to have washed off
it.

I went down the path and across the flat grass it stood on,
and sat on the top step just inside and put my head against
the iron post. The flower-beds were getting very tatty-look-
ing and the grass was muddy with puddles forming in it.
Like a shabby old meadow. There was an awful smell of
men's lavatories and one of the stacked-up metal chairs had
fallen to bits on the floor. Someone had drawn hearts with
arrows through on the floor and there was a bundle of fish-
and-chip papers, transparent with dark grease in a corner.
Near to my face on the post someone had written a foul
word in very perfect letters.

The rain pattered down on the roof and the grass and the
ruins of the flower-beds, and the dismal old garlic and the
tall sad trees and prickled the beck and spattered the sea,
and the fat barrage-balloon on the cliffs up above and the
men looking after it and the fields beyond and then the
moors and then the mountains, wet and sodden and grey
for evermore. It drenched my bare legs sticking out of the
bandstand, and my socks and my brown lace-ups.

I suppose I sat there for a very long time. Far, far away
I knew that the rest of the world was going on. If I'd tried
I think I could have imagined it all – people sitting,
breathing, telling each other things, shouting at each
other, nodding at each other over teacups, narrowing their
eyes and pointing guns at each other, looking at their
watches, lighting the gas. Mother spinning round the
kitchen saying to Rowley, 'Heavens, Jess'll be in in a

minute and no tea. Don't move one inch while I fly out for the kippers.'

But I wasn't going to try, and I sat on and on.

Once above me through the sea-wood some boys went running, shouting and making noises at each other like guns, and then an old man in a macintosh with a dog. He called to the dog. Then it was all quiet again. Then Miss Philemon came walking through the wood in a pixie hood and a waterproof cape and carrying her case of books in front of her in both hands like Little Red Riding Hood.

'Stop this,' I said. 'This is the sort of thing I can't stand. It's on the edge of *enjoying* people dying.'

Perhaps she's right and everything I see is out of focus, I thought. It's funny Walter de la Mare didn't spot it though if it's true. It was a terrible poem. It *was* a terrible poem. But there was one thing good about it – the idea was good, the idea of the maniac was good. Walter de la Mare would have understood that.

But would he? Did anybody really see anything the same as anybody else? Rowley could tell the difference between even little bits of cars, but he couldn't understand different angles. 'My right is your *left*,' you had to keep saying. My right is everybody else's left. The rain stopped and I still sat on and on and on, and it began to grow dark.

I said to myself, 'I am here but I am nothing. I see nothing. I know nothing. Whenever I think I know, I don't. It's always lies. What I see turns out to have been always fancy. It's "Oh, Jessica!", "For goodness' sake, Jessica!", "Poor old Jessica!", "Jessica's a bit off her nut."' Just when you think someone's thinking like you do, they give you a blank look and can't remember.

'I'm all alone,' I thought, 'I'm utterly, utterly alone.' I said it out loud and started howling a bit and got up and walked back up through the wood. When I got to the gates I looked back into the trees and shouted, 'There's nobody there, there's nobody there.' A woman – a frightful-looking woman in one of those awful musquash coats with a filthy old peke trailing along behind her turned her face on me and opened her eyes in fright. They stuck out a bit, like eggs. But I didn't bother. Nobody was going to interest me. She was nothing. I was alone.

I hauled the picture along back to the station somehow and saw the station-master's ghastly old trousers-bottoms as I got to the barrier. 'Best come this way,' he said and took me round by the gate for the luggage. I saw the arc the bolt makes on the station floor and his poor old waddly shoes with the toes turning up. But I put them out of my head. He wasn't going to interest me.

There was a train in, and I heaved the picture on to the floor of an empty carriage, shoved it along between the seats and got in after it. The station-master was watching with his horrible purple lip hanging down – I didn't bother to look, for I knew – and came shambling along and laid his chin on the window.

'Tha's late,' he said.

'I've got permission.'

'Yon's a great thing. Orter be int van.'

I tried to look over his head because I knew I was utterly

alone. Everyone in this world was utterly alone. And I had a pain in my stomach.

'No chips today then?' he said and stood back to wave his arm to the guard. I saw he had a sort of look in his eye and I got a bit of a shock because just in the glance I got I thought it was a kind look – almost sort of merry – and before I could stop myself I thought of Rupert Brooke saying, 'I must love every greasy button . . .' But I soon stopped.

'It's no good loving,' I said to the horses on the floor. 'No good comes of loving.' I rolled the orange round and round, first into one eye-socket, then into the other. 'Actually,' I thought, 'it was a bit snobbish to pick out *work-men*. He meant everyone – he ought to have loved everyone's buttons. Clerks' buttons, schoolmasters' buttons, that old bird in the musquash coat's buttons. If you have to remind yourself to love dirty old *workmen's* buttons, then you don't really.' I wondered about the types of buttons that Dickens and poor old Thomas Hardy loved. Or maybe they didn't.

The train stopped now and then and a few people got in and out. Some of them gave me looks. One of them said, 'Orter be int van, yon,' and pointed at the picture (I'd got it on the opposite seat now). Another man – a soldier – sat and looked at it for a bit. He joggled back and forward just look-ing at it. I looked at it too, rolling and rolling the orange, watching them, the horsemen, pacing around on the bright pink grass. (It's grass, not sand and blowing about.) 'What's it meant to be when it's at 'ome?' the workman asked, and another man in overalls said, 'It's that Picasso, likely,' and they both laughed and looked at me, but I didn't say anything.

I'd really got into a very funny mood by this time and when we got to Cleveland Sands station – my station – I surprised myself by not getting out. I just sat on. I felt all kinds of things watching me – God, I suppose, and my conscience and everything, and I just said, as if it were Miss LeBouche, 'I'm not going home. I don't want to.'

'Where are you going?' asked God, puzzled. Quite nice.

'I don't know.'

'All right,' He said.

'I'm going to Dunedin Street,' I said. 'I'm taking the picture to those people.'

I felt better at once. I realized suddenly how much I longed to see them. 'Well I never!' she'd say, and put up her hands in the air. 'Well look who's here,' and she'd begin laughing. 'Come over, lass, come 'ere.' She would really want to see me that woman, and Ern and the old man. In fact I couldn't think why I'd only just thought of it.

22

We reached Shields East in about three quarters of an hour and by the time we arrived, except for this pain in my stomach, I was feeling better – much more comfortable and sort of pleased with myself. I knew they would be there. 'It takes a crane to move me,' she had said. I knew I hadn't got *her* out of focus anyway. I was utterly sure of that.

What's more I was absolutely certain that she wanted me to go and see her. She had stretched her arms out. She was so lovely and fat. She just sat there all day feeling happy, laughing at whatever happened even when the street fell down, fussing about nothing. 'And whatever did you want to go there for?' I heard mother's voice, her hair all wild. I sniffed and looked out at the darkness through a scratch in the black window blind and thought of the horsemen hanging up in Dunedin Street.

But then, after a while, I decided that they – the fat woman and the other two – wouldn't really want the picture much. I just knew it suddenly. They'd be polite, of course, but if I really thought about it, they wouldn't really think a lot of it. After I'd gone they might even laugh at it. 'I know,' I said, 'I'll give them the cheque. I can tell them how to use it. You must take it to a bank and say it is a present and get given money for it.' They would be very pleased to have some money, and I had very little need of any extra money. There were clothes – but it didn't look as if I'd be asked to High Thwaite again.

I waited till all the workmen had got out and gone through the barrier at Shields East and then I asked the ticket collector if I could leave the picture for a little while behind his sentry-box. He gave me a queer look.

'Where you goin'?'

'Just into Shields East.'

'Let's have a look at that pass.'

I remembered my pass and got it out of my gas-mask.

'That's a lot of good,' he said. 'It's between Cleveland Sands and Cleveland Spa. It's got nowt to do wi' Shields East. You'll have ter pay.'

'I've no money,' I said, and remembered the cheque. 'Oh yes I have but it's a cheque. As a matter of fact I was going to give it to someone . . .'

He examined the cheque carefully.

'What's this then?' he said at last. 'Twenty pounds from *The Times* newspaper – are you tellin' me it's thine?'

'Yes it is. It's for something I've written.'

'In *The Times* newspaper?'

'Yes.'

'And yer goin' ter give it to someone in Shields East?'

'Yes.'

He stared at me very hard.

'Some friends in Dunedin Street,' I said.

He pointed a big finger at me and kept it steady like a gun. 'Oho,' he said, 'I knew I'd seen thee afore. It was thee and yon lad as was 'ere the Sunday. The Sunday Dunedin Street copped it'

I just glared.

'Off,' he said. 'Go on – off. You're not goin' to Dunedin Street tonight, and for why? a) because you 'aven't no money to leave the station and b) because it's time you was in bed and c) because Dunedin Street's not there no more. It's three parts down and t'other part empty. Evacuated. Not a living soul left. Off 'ome with thee to Cleveland Sands.'

So I took the picture and got it under the subway and sat on the platform opposite, waiting for a train home, and every now and then he fastened a dreadful look on me from over the line. It seemed rather a slack time in the evening and no tickets to punch.

In the end I got home to Cleveland Sands and pulled the picture out with me – and then found I'd left the orange. So I laid the picture flat on the station platform and got back in and found it under the seat among the pipes; and got out again just as the train began to move off. If I hadn't got out I'd have been carried back to school again, to Cleveland Spa. I felt rather dizzy and wondered how long I could travel up and down the line before anybody noticed. One could almost live on trains, I thought, it would be a nice easy way to live except for eating. The pain in my stomach was really rather bad.

I picked up the picture and dragged it over to the wooden steps that went up over the line and propped it up against them. Then I sat down on the bottom step and put my hands on my stomach. I was surprised to see how dirty they were. The orange was very dirty, too, and my socks that had got so wet were filthy. And looking at the orange I realized what the pain was – I was most terribly hungry. It seemed quite a few days ago that I'd had the stew and semolina at the fourpenny dinner, and what with everyone beaming and smiling at me I hadn't eaten much. It must be long past tea-time now. As a matter of fact it seemed to be quite dark. The station lights were on – blue lights. The bulbs were all painted navy blue with a little hole left in the bottom making everything look like hell.

'Well, I'd rather go home,' I thought, and I leaned against the railing of the bridge and looked at a sort of machine that stood at the foot of the steps. We used to play with it last year, when we were little, while we were waiting in the mornings for the train. It was a Novelty Machine – it said so on a little brass plate on the side: 'Novelty Machines, Inc. Stratford upon Avon, Warwicks.' You had to put sixpence in – it was expensive – and turn a pointer on a sort of clock-face with letters on it and you could punch out your name and address up to thirty letters. Then you pulled the most enormous handle and a metal plate shot out that you could nail up outside your front door – your name and address or anything. Her Majesty, J. Vye or anything.

It was a very queer-looking machine on four bandy legs. Cabriolet legs. Oli, olé legs. And I saw for the first time that they had *feet*. Like a bird. Four claws each clutching a ball. Four of them. And it seemed to me so silly and funny to think of someone making that machine with those feet, someone in Stratford upon Avon, every day making those birds' feet, hundreds and hundreds of them. Every day, going off in the morning, taking his cap off the hallstand, ''Bye then, Else, I'm off,' and just making those feet 'though I don't suppose he'd be doing that now,' I thought, 'he'd be in the army.

'What you do in Civvy Street then, Bill?' 'Made feet' . . . I suddenly felt absolutely, completely happy thinking about it. I just gazed and gazed. And then I found I was gazing down – high up above in the station roof and there I was all of a heap on the bottom step with the picture beside me and that marvellous, beautiful machine, throwing out its chest like a hero.

I looked a poor thing, flopped down beside it and there was someone running up to me – in fact a whole lot of people in a fandango, their arms and legs waving about, their hair on end and their hands and feet flapping. Big ones and small ones, all running: and I thought those crazy people seem to be in a fine old state.

And Rowley had his hands round my knees and was butting me on the shoulder with his head (his head is absolutely fantastic – it's as hard as a calf) and there was mother crying and father biffing one hand into the other like a pestle and mortar and behind them a whole lot more – the sidesman in the ticket office and (crikey!) Miss LeBouche, and a policeman and Florence and Mrs Baxter, and half the world.

Mother looked lovely actually. 'Oh, Jessica, Jessica! It's eleven o'clock at night!'

Honestly the fuss they made.

The curious thing is that in the morning I couldn't have felt more ordinary and quiet. I'd got tonsillitis. That was the first thing my mother had said on the station after all the carry-on (and I thought at the time, trust her!). 'This will mean tonsillitis tomorrow,' she said. She was still weeping and crying and going on, yet she had to say that.

Anyway she was right and I caught it and a high temperature: but it didn't matter because I felt so happy. My father went over to the vicarage and got *The Times*, and there it was – rather in a corner and hardly any margin, but still. It had JESSICA VYE at the bottom.

As a matter of fact the poem is not as bad as I thought. I managed to read it through very fast and it didn't make me feel as sick as I'd expected. Being printed was a big improvement. Actually I looked it over several times during the morning.

Next day there was the most gigantic post – letters from Giles and Magdalene and one from Mrs F-S saying 'we knew the Masefields at Andover', whatever that means, and from all sorts of odd bods we hadn't heard of since my father became a curate. There was a sort of thin, letter-card thing ending, 'love, Christian' – very childish writing – and a great screed from the headmistress of the posh kindergarten, and a postcard with a tank on, beautifully written and signed 'Iris'.

And then in the middle of the morning a telegram – the first I have ever had, and it set Mother shaking though she hadn't even got a *cousin* in the war. I ask you! It said 'Magnificent stop Congratulations stop I was right stop Hanger.' And father said, 'Who on *earth* is that? What a most unfortunate name. Is his first one coat?' and they laughed.

But, like at the Novelty Machine, I just felt filled with love, knowing that good things take place.

FAITH FOX

Jane Gardam

'Terribly funny and clever . . . the best thing she's done'
Victoria Wood

When sweet, healthy, hearty Holly Fox dies suddenly in childbirth, the Surrey village whose pearl she was reverberates with shock. She leaves behind her a helpless, silent husband, and a tiny daughter, Faith. Everyone assumes Holly's loving and capable mother Thomasina will look after Faith, but when she unaccountably deserts her newborn grandchild, the baby must be packed off to her father's peculiar family in the North – 'the very strangest people you ever saw, my dear'.

With wisdom, generosity and understanding, Jane Gardam takes as her subject the English heart in all its eccentric variety. *Faith Fox* sheds a clear, true light on the misery of bereavement and the joyous possibility of a new beginning.

'*Faith Fox* has quite as sharp a take on modern times as *Trainspotting* . . .
if you're too hip for Jane Gardam, then you're too hip'
D. J. Taylor, *New Statesman*

'Brilliant . . . brilliant . . . brilliant' A. N. Wilson, *Evening Standard*

'Each character in its crowded cast leaps to life . . .
A captivating tale' *Sunday Telegraph*

'Funny and admirable . . . Jane Gardam writes with a dark and buoyant energy which continually challenges and provokes' *The Times*

ABACUS
978-0-349-12101-7

THE QUEEN OF THE TAMBOURINE

Jane Gardam

Winner of the Costa/Whitbread Novel of the Year

'Moving, written with an assured elegance and very funny'
Daily Telegraph

Eliza Peabody is a dangerous – if blameless – do-gooder. She is too enthusiastic; she talks too much. Her concern for the welfare of the inhabitants of her south London road extends to annoying, albeit well-meaning, notes of unsolicited advice under their doors.

It is just such a one-sided correspondence that heralds Eliza's undoing. Did her letter have something to do with her neighbour's abrupt disappearance? Why will no one else speak of her? And why the watchful, pitying looks and embarrassment that now greet the still beautiful, bountiful Eliza on her errands of mercy?

By hilarious and disturbing stages we watch Eliza Peabody inch her way into suburban Siberia. And still more dark surprises lie in wait as, gradually and bewitchingly, black comedy transforms itself into psychological thriller.

'A startling portrait of a woman who is dying alive. You not only laugh at, but with Eliza, and understand her sense of apartness. By the end of this brilliant book, you feel that you have known her all your life'
Sunday Times

ABACUS
978-0-349-10226-9

GOD ON THE ROCKS

Jane Gardam

During one glorious summer between the wars the realities of life and the sexual ritual dance of the adult world creep into the life of young Margaret Marsh. Her father, preaching the doctrine of the unsavoury Primal Saints; her mother, bitterly nostalgic for what might have been; Charles and Binkie, anchored in the past and a game of words; dying Mrs Frayling and Lydia the maid, given to the vulgar enjoyment of life: all contribute to Margaret's shattering moment of truth. And when the storm breaks, it is not only God who is on the rocks as the summer hurtles towards drama, tragedy, and a touch of farce.

'Jane Gardam has a spectacular gift for detail of the local and period kind, and for details which make characters so subtly unpredictable that they ring true' *TLS*

'Exact, piquant and comical' *Observer*

'Marvellous . . .a wonder' *Vogue*

ABACUS
978-0-349-12149-9

OLD FILTH

Jane Gardam

Shortlisted for the Orange Prize 2005

FILTH, in his heyday, was an international lawyer with a practice in the Far East. Now only the oldest QCs and Silks can remember that his nickname stood for Failed In London Try Hong Kong.

Long ago, Old Filth was a Raj orphan – one of the many young children sent 'Home' from the East to be fostered and educated in England. This novel tells his story, from his birth in what was then Malaya to the extremities of his old age. In so doing, Jane Gardam not only encapsulates a whole period from the glory days of the British Empire, through the Second World War, to the present and beyond, but she also illuminates the complexities of the character known variously as Eddie, the Judge, Fevvers, Filth, Master of the Inner Temple, Teddy and Sir Edward Feathers.

'A magnificent, deeply moving and compassionate portrait of an era and a sentimental education. Please read it' *Daily Mail*

'This novel is surely Gardam's masterpiece. On the human level, it is one of the most moving fictions I have read for years' *Guardian*

'Beautiful, vivid and defiantly funny' *The Times*

ABACUS
978-0-349-11840-6

To buy any of our books and to find out
more about Abacus and Little, Brown, our authors
and titles, as well as events and book clubs,
visit our website

www.littlebrown.co.uk

and follow us on Twitter

@AbacusBooks
@LittleBrownUK

To order any Abacus titles p & p free in the UK,
please contact our mail order supplier on:

+ 44 (0)1832 737525

Customers not based in the UK should contact
the same number for appropriate postage
and packing costs.